I0566601

BIZARRE TALES OF HORROR

A Paranormal Horror Anthology

edited by J. Thayer McKinney

Cedar Loft Publishing

Petersburg, West Virginia

Cedar Loft Publishing
PO Box 1125
Petersburg, WV 26847
www.clpublishing.net

Publisher's Note: This is a work of fiction. Names, characters, places, and incidents are a product of the author's imagination. Locales and public names are sometimes used for atmospheric purposes. Any resemblance to actual people, living or dead, or to businesses, companies, events, institutions, or locales is completely coincidental.

Book Layout ©2015 BookDesignTemplates.com

Cover Design - SelfPubBookCovers.com/RavenandBlack

Bizarre Tales of Horror -- 1st ed.
ISBN 978-0-6925404-1-1

CONTENTS

INTRODUCTION

If you love a frightening horror story, in Bizarre Tales of Horror, you will find twelve stories that are sure to satisfy your craving for a good scare. The stories presented in Bizarre Tales of Horror are written by extremely talented writers who have a vivid imagination and are adept at spinning terrifying tales.

Have you ever thought about where your thoughts, dreams, nightmares, and imagination originates? It's my thought that nothing is original, everything has been experienced or we couldn't think it, dream it, or imagine it. With that thought in mind, where did these tales actually come from in the writer's imagination? Are they forgotten memories, memories transferred down through the ages through DNA, or are they glimpses of another dimension?

You be the judge.

J. Thayer McKinney ~~ Editor of Bizarre Tales of Horror

A BIG SPLASH

Patrick McKinney

Meet Rolland Pratt, a small statured man with a slight build and sharp, birdlike features. Rolland grew up in near poverty, in the mountains of southern West Virginia but he has always been determined to, as he would call it, make "a big splash". Unfortunately for Rolland his eighth grade education and lack of good judgment seems to always work against him.

Finally Rolland gets the break he's been wanting. He's gotten out of his small hometown and landed a job with a major company in the city. The company, Quantum Applications, is a government and military contractor developing high tech hardware and devices, including time technology. Rolland was able to get a position as night janitor in the time technology section of Building B on the Quantum Applications main campus.

Monday through Friday, Rolland clocks in at 10:00 PM and works until 6:00 AM the next morning. All night he sweeps and mops floors, empties trash cans, and cleans restrooms. On one particular night right after clocking in he sees his friend William who happens to be working late. William is one of the scientists in time technology. He grew up in the same county as Rolland so he understands Rolland's upbringing. William feels sorry for Rolland when the other employees makes fun of him or badgers him. To make Rolland feel comfortable William has developed a friendship with him.

This night William is working late perfecting a small device the department has been working on for several months. He showed it to Rolland. The device looks like a cellphone but William explains it's a time portal. He makes Rolland promise to not mention the device to anyone and goes on to tell him more about it. With the device the developers at Quantum Applications plan to one day be able to travel back in time and then return to the present. So far they haven't been able to develop a test to verify the person using the device actually went back in time. The entire time William is explaining the time portal Rolland's eyes are lit up. He feels like a child that has found a new toy.

"Golly how's that thingy work?" Rolland asks.

William shows Rolland the keypad and explains, "Once it's working you set the time you want to visit, then you press the green button to be transported."

Then he points to the red button and says, "You press this button when you are ready to transport back to present time."

Rolland wants to see for himself and starts to grab for the device but William pulls back and says, "Sorry, but this is a prototype and can't be handled by just anyone."

Just then from another part of the building a voice rings out, "PRATT! Where are you?" It was Rolland's shift leader. Rolland immediately runs out of the lab and down the hall to get back to work.

Later that week Roland is sitting in his room waiting to go to work and thinking about the device William had showed him. He knows this could be his ticket to the easy life but how would he do it.

While he is sitting and thinking he looks out his second floor window across the street at the neighborhood market. The owner is changing the lottery sign to show the prize is now up to over 400 million dollars. Watching, Rolland thought to himself how great it would be to have all that money. Then it hit him, the drawing is at 8:00 PM Friday the 14th. All he needed to do is get the numbers before going to work. Then use the time portal to go back to Thursday, buy a ticket, then return to Friday and collect his millions! He is so excited he can barely control himself.

When Friday arrives Rolland gets to work on time and immediately starts to work like nothing is going to happen. At about 11:30 PM, when he's certain everyone has left for the weekend; he makes his way to the lab and gets the time portal.

Once he has it, he goes to the janitor closet so security won't notice him. He walks into the closet and closes the door. He's just about the figure out how to activate the portal when he sees he forgot to turn the water off in the mop tub on the floor. With its slow drain it has started overflowing soapy water onto the floor.

Rolland reaches over to turn off the water but he slips on the soapy floor. Trying to catch himself, reflex causes him to simultaneously press most of the buttons on the portal with his thumb. At this point everything goes blank!

"'e's comin' 'round!"

Rolland is holding and massaging his head between both hands. His eyes come into focus and he sees several men standing around him. Startled he jumps and looks around. He's lying in what looks to be the lower bed of a bunk bed or something and these young men are watching him.

"Easy man," they tell him. "You're one lucky bloke! That was a terrible spill you took during all the ruckus."

Rolland sat up and got his bearings. "Where am I?" he asks.

One of the men replies, "Cabin E-41, where are your people. They have to be worried. You've been out a few hours. We figured you had a few pints and brought you in here to sleep it off."

Rolland is still trying to figure out what is going on. He doesn't recognize these men.

How did they get in the building? Does security know they're here? Will he be in trouble for having these guys here?

Just then the door to the room flies open and another man sticks his head in and shouts, "Get your valuables together and get topside straight away! The water, it's coming up the corridor ask I speak!"

The men grabbed some things and shoved Rolland out the doorway into the hall. They fell into the flow of people moving down the hallway and up a set of steps.

At this point Rolland is completely lost. Worried he has missed the lottery cutoff he asks what the date is. One of the men blurted out it is the 15th, just a couple of hours past midnight.

Relieved, Rolland told them he needed to get a ticket before he did anything else.

The men looked at him and they all began to laugh and one said as they came to a closed door,

"Blimey, are you daft? You needed a ticket to board the ship!"

Through the door they all stepped out onto the deck of the ship. There were what looked to be hundreds of other people there too. Many were crying, others stood in shock as to be expecting an impending doom.

"Ship? What ship?" Rolland asks.

All the men point over to the round life preserver hanging on the wall. "That ship," they say in unison.

Rolland turns to read the name printed on the doughnut shaped preserver. The bottom read LIVERPOOL. And the top, TITANIC. Just then he felt the deck beneath him begin listing forward very sharply. Shaking and beginning to cry Rolland screams, "What time is it?"

One of the men yells out, "Quarter past two." Then the mighty ship trembles as Rolland's consciousness fades and the ship slips below the dark icy water just as everything goes black.

"Where did all this water come from?" someone exclaimed. Oh, no, it's Rolland!"

Several of the early employees coming in Monday morning find Rolland face down in the overflowing mop tub.

They pull him out and onto the floor but it's too late. From his condition and appearance they can only assume he has been submerged the entire weekend.

One of the workers looks in the tub and notices something that had been under Rolland. "What is that?" he says.

William looks in the tub and reaches in to get the time portal. "I wonder how that got in there?" someone asks.

Another worker replies, "Well it's ruined now and it was the prototype, the only one."

William consoled them all explaining, "It doesn't matter about the time portal. That entire operation has been scrubbed. We can't prove we can actually go back so the government pulled the plug on the spending for it."

"I guess we just weren't meant to be able to cheat time."

About the author

Patrick McKinney was born and raised in Ohio, has traveled throughout the United States and Canada, and currently resides in Virginia. He enjoys writing, photography, and traveling. He is currently working on his first novel, yet to be named, and hopes to publish it within the next year.

~~ © 2015 A Big Splash/Patrick McKinney

BIZARRE TALES OF HORROR

DOWN IN ONE ROUND

Nick Nafpliotis

Michael Corson wasn't sure how long he'd been out when the sound of the old woman chanting awakened him.

The last thing he remembered was getting swarmed by Sam Mansi and the rest of Mr. Abbatiello's goons on his way home from the bar.

Once they surrounded him, Corson had figured that was it. They'd either whack him right there or take him to a more discreet location to do the deed. At the very least, he'd expected to find himself inside of a trunk or with a bag over his head.

Instead, he now found himself bound upright in the back of a large van. Next to him was an ancient looking woman dressed completely in red. Her head was adorned with something that appeared to be a shark skull and deer antlers. She was also murmuring the same phrase over and over again while rattling a small collection of bones inside her outstretched left hand.

In front of him, two enforcers whom he'd only seen a few times sat rigidly facing front. Mansi was further up in the front passenger seat next to the driver, whom he'd never seen before.

"What the hell is this, Mansi?" Corson muttered as the fuzziness in his head slowly morphed into a sharp pain. "You guys gonna do this old school...take me down to the docks and all that? Or maybe you're going to cut me up into little pieces and feed me to some rabid dogs or something. No one does that type of sick stuff anymore, though. Not even your senile old boss, Abbatiello."

"He'd actually prefer to do much worse than either of those to you," Mansi replied calmly while staring out the car window.

"Yeah, well he won't," Corson snapped back, tasting the blood in his mouth for the first time. "You know this means war, right? Scaletta protects his people."

"Unfortunately for you, Mr. Scaletta seems to be doing a pretty terrible job of that at the moment," Mansi replied with the slightest hint of a grin on his face.

Carson swore and began rocking in his seat, desperately trying to break out of the zip ties around his wrists and ankles. After it became obvious that his efforts were for naught, he turned his attention to the old woman adorned in the bizarre animal skull helmet, who was still chanting and rattling the bones in her hand.

"And just what the hell is her problem, anyway?" Corson hissed at Mansi while still looking at her. "Is Abbatiello's taste in whores starting to go a little wonky or something?"

When no one replied, Corson turned his attention to the side window, trying to see if he could determine where they were from their surroundings. To his surprise, the area they were driving through did not appear to be any sort of urban landscape. The road signs indicated that they were on Highway 11 in the upper part of New York State. Once they passed Rouses Point and turned onto Highway 2, however, he knew exactly where they were headed.

"Vermont?" Corson said incredulously. "Are you guys going to wine and dine me at a nice bed and breakfast before putting a bullet through my head?"

None of the passengers replied. As they crossed the state line and headed toward the small islands that dotted Lake Champlain, Corson began to suspect how they were going to get rid of him...even if it didn't make sense.

"Really, you guys are that cliché?" he said with a laugh. "Dumping a body in Lake Champlain. How original. I hope you brought cement shoes and all that, too. Wouldn't want to fall short of all the mob stereotypes now, would we?"

"We're not drowning you," Mansi coolly replied. "You'll be getting something much better."

"And what would that be, if I may be so bold to ask?"

"You get to meet The Champ."

There was a moment of confused silence before Carson burst into laughter.

"Are you freaking serious?" he exclaimed between breaths. "You guys are driving me all the way across state lines to meet some torture expert who names himself like a bad character from an 80's movie? Do you idiots not realize how royally screwed all of you are once Scaletta finds out about this."

"He won't, because no one will even remember who you are," Mansi said while looking at his phone. "Not even us."

"Up yours," Corson shot back, resigned to finish the rest of the ride in silence while he tried to figure out a means of escape.

By the time they got to Grand Isle State Park, however, he'd only managed to add a searing pain in his wrists to go along with the one on the back of his head where the goons had knocked him out. When they stopped the men came around to pull him out of the van, his bites and furious wriggling was met with two quick punches to the face, temporarily stunning Corson into stillness.

The goons carried him over to the edge of Lake Champlain while Mansi stood by and watched. A few feet behind them, the old woman continued the same chant while stretching one of her hands out into the air. Her other hand was still shaking and swirling the small bones, which rattled so feverishly now that it was almost as if they'd been electrified.

"So what's next?" Corson said after spitting out a bloody tooth. "Are you guys gonna bring in some type of voodoo priest to take my heart out of my chest while Harrison Ford watches from the trees?"

Instead of answering, the men who'd carried him onto the beach went back to the van and pulled out a large wooden raft.

Mansi walked up to the old woman, who'd finally stopped chanting, and handed her a wad of cash while pointing towards a sedan that was parked nearby.

"Once again, Roberta, Mr. Abbatiello greatly appreciates your services. As usual, the rental car contains one first class plane ticket back to Charleston. Your flight leaves in eight hours from LaGuardia Airport."

"Roberta?!" Corson yelled from his prone position on the ground. "You got a witch whose name is 'Roberta'...and you flew her in from Charleston? Abbatiello really is losing it, isn't he?!"

Corson attempted to force a confident cackle through his swollen lips as the goons brought the raft over towards him. When he glanced back at the old woman, he saw her looking back at him as she got into the rental car.

For the first time since he'd woken up, she wasn't chanting or fiddling with bones. Instead, the woman was looking directly at him with an expression that almost seemed like pity. Before he could say or shout anything to her, however, she'd gotten into the car and driven off, leaving him to be lifted by Abbatiello's men onto the raft.

"Okay, seriously," Corson pleaded as they dropped the bound wooden poles into the water, "at least have the decency to tell me how I'm going to die."

"We're putting you in the ring with The Champ... and we're even going to give you a fighting chance," Mansi said as he tossed a knife down beside him.

"What the hell is this?!" Corson shouted back. "Why can't you errand boys just do me like a man?! What the hell are you sending me out onto Lake Champlain to fight?!"

"Like I said before, you're stepping into the ring with The Champ," Mansi calmly replied. "He's very old and set in his ways, which includes having his offerings alive so they can try to escape...although no one ever does."

"First time for everything," Corson replied as he scooted across the raft and grabbed the knife.

"It may have happened before us, but we keep records now," Mansi said as the goons began walking back to the van. "And during our partnership with The Champ, the people we send out to him are always beaten. This not only gets rid of Mr. Abbatiello's problem, but also makes it disappear for good. No one will remember you. No one will ever know you existed. The only proof that you were ever alive will be in our possession, where it will stay locked up forever...or until the next round of doc shredding, at least."

"What the hell are you even talking about?" Corson said as he began sawing at the zip tie around his wrists.

Mansi, however, didn't respond this time. Instead, he checked his phone, turned around, and headed back towards the van.

After he got in, the vehicle pulled away and disappeared down the road, leaving Corson alone in the middle of the lake.

"Old Man Abbatiello's really losing it," Corson muttered to himself as the zip tie around his hands finally snapped in two.

Corson's mind wanted to try and wrap itself around the bizarre circumstances that led to him floating on a raft by himself in the middle of Lake Champlain, but the seemingly easy path to freedom became the sole focus of his hands.

The zip tie at his ankles came off much more easily, but still took long enough that by the time he was done, the raft had gotten a few hundred feet from shore. He was just about to dive into the water when something bumped the raft from underneath. Corson paused, looking behind him where a ripple surged in the water from the other direction.

"What the hell was that?" he muttered under his breath.

As if in response, another bump came from below the raft, this time nearly knocking him into the water. Corson brought his feet back over bound wooden poles, looking down to see what was beneath him.

In the next instant, he found himself flying through the air. Beneath him, the raft had splintered into a million pieces.

A hiss followed by a loud roar followed Corson upwards, causing him to shriek in fear. He looked down just in time to see what appeared to be a giant set of antlers attached to an impossibly large set of jaws.

Before he could makes any sense out of what his eyes were seeing, Corson crashed back down into the water. He quickly forced himself up to the surface, where a long, snaking mass was rushing in his direction. Corson swore and began swimming towards the shore. He only managed to get a few feet away before a set of sharp teeth clamped down around his right leg. In one swift motion, he was jerked through the air and tossed back towards the middle of the lake.

Corson bobbed up to the surface more slowly this time, the place where his leg had been bitten now bleeding profusely. As his vision faded and his head swirled, one word kept repeating itself over and over again in his head.

Champ.

He hadn't even considered the first possibility that popped into his head because of how ridiculous it was. People always spoke about the legendary monster of Lake Champlain as if it were a joke rather than a something that could actually exist. Sightings of the creature had been reported for centuries, but all they ever ended up being were large pieces of driftwood or tourists with terrible Photoshop skills. Now, however, the enormous serpent was headed back in his direction, cresting out of the water as it got closer.

"How has no one ever seen this?" Corson thought as he struggled to keep his eyes open.

When the creature was close, it reared up out of the lake and curled its neck back. The antlers on its long, narrow head made the serpent appear to be a complete abomination of nature. Nothing that looked like that existed. Nothing that looked like that should exist.

As it peered down at Corson and cocked its nightmarish head to one side, however, he finally understood why no one had ever seen it...and why no one ever would.

Champ's eyes glowed red in the night, burning through his struggling vision right to his very soul. A pain overtook him like he'd never experienced before. It wasn't one of bones breaking for flesh splitting, though. This was his very life being extinguished.

Corson's body went rigid as the creature's head moved in closer to his. He felt everything disappearing; his memories, his identity, even his will to live. Champ pulled back for a moment, giving him a brief respite from the cold nothingness that had permeated through his entire being. The sliver of peace he'd felt was then quickly interrupted by a terrible roar, the creature's jaws opening so far that it looked as if they might come unhinged.

A second later, Champ snapped forward, biting down over the lifeless mass of flesh and bone that was drifting in front of him. The creature then coiled once above the water before silently diving back into the depths of Lake Champlain.

An hour later, a single large piece of driftwood floated to the lake's surface, adding a calm coda to the frantic murder that had taken place such a short time ago. Back in New York, Abbatiello's organization would find that they were in possession of files and records on a man who never even existed. The only natural evidence of what occurred that night on the lake was an object that now floated aimlessly in the moonlight.

About the author

Nick Nafpliotis is a music teacher and writer from Charleston, South Carolina. During the day, he instructs students from the ages of 11-14 on how to play band instruments. At night, he writes about weird crime, bizarre history, pop culture, and humorous classroom experiences on his blog, RamblingBeachCat.com. He is a television, novel, and comic book reviewer for AdventuresinPoorTaste.com. You can also follow Nick on Twitter where he brings shame to his family on a daily basis.

Previous Credits

Publication at T. Gene Davis Speculative Fiction Blog

Publication in Dead Harvest anthology from Scarlett Galleon Publications

Publication in NonBinary Review

Publication in Horror in Bloom anthology by Visionary Press Collaborative

Publication at Perihelion Online Science Fiction Magazine

Publication in Fear's Accomplice: Halloween anthology by Noodle Doodle Publications

Publication in Terror at the Beach anthology by Noodle Doodle Publications

Publication in Mad Scientist Journal
Publication in Black Treacle
Publication in Wicked Words Quarterly
Publication in Literary Hatchet
Publication at Voluted Tales_
Publication in Pithy Pages_
Publication in Nebula Rift

HOURGLASS

Kenneth Goldman

"Time goes, you say? Ah, no! Alas, Time stays, we go."
~~ Henry Austin Dobson

"It strikes! one, two,
Three, four, five, six.
Enough, enough, dear watch,
Thy pulse hath beat enough."
~~Ben Johnson

Howard removed the hourglass from his mantel, and placing it on the table he watched the grains shift. He had bought the object - a 'grotesque egg timer,' Camille once had called it – at some roadside flea market for fifteen bills. Yes, it was cheap and the gizmo looked cheaper with the winged cherub clinging to it, a golden Cupid with arrow in hand. But there was something almost sensual about the piece, something womanly with its figure-eight shape and an erotic symmetry as its contents shifted.

Beautiful, really. And a little sad too. Because when you thought about it, the passage of time was always a little sad.

Howard recalled some genius once saying that the only thing constant in life is change. Like those shifting sands, time had altered things significantly with Camille. Similar to that tacky "Days of Our Lives" tag line – the soaper was one Camille never missed – like sands through an hourglass these were the days of Howard Jamison's life, all right. He watched every grain shift from top to bottom as he had watched those days of his life with Camille spill through his fingers.

During their early times, falling in love happened easily. The young man's electrified hormones overpowered his reason from the moment he noticed how nicely one golden haired Rutgers coed could fill out her ass tugging mini. For Howard that red hot emotion required a full thirteen minutes past "Hello" inside an upscale Manhattan pub, the time needed for Camille Dorsey to finish her merlot and flash a 100 watt smile his way. With a simple touch of her hand Howard felt his heart race, felt the muscles of his groin throb. If she would have allowed it, he would have taken the young woman right there on the bar's counter, sending the beer mugs and wine glasses flying. But he had waited maybe four weeks before the two officially sealed the deal with breathless promises moaned beneath Howard's sheets.

"Oh God, Camille, I'll always love you!" His words just spilled out bypassing his brain completely, a new experience for the young accountant whose usual thoughts required mathematical precision. Then, music to the ears of a young man in love...

"Yes, Oh yes..."

Beautiful and sad, the memories. Maybe behind everything beautiful lurked sadness. Howard watched the hourglass' shifting grains, remembering an early fantasy from those golden days.

Camille wears a uniform from her Parochial school years, one of those Catholic girl's kilt-like skirts with a crisp white blouse and green knee socks. But the skirt is rolled all the way up and young Camille's very white panties are fully exposed. Howard reaches for the warm spot beneath them. Camille protests, of course, but her objection lacks earnestness and lasts only for a moment. Noticing the hint of moisture in the material, Howard savors a faint and wonderful whiff of femininity just before he takes her.

With no coaxing from him, the memories came. As an adolescent Camille had attended Our Sisters of Mercy School for Girls. Most males would have considered the green plaid skirt and drab knee socks as unflattering and ugly, but not Howard. Through his adulthood he would have selected that Camille wear her Catholic Girl's School uniform over anything from Victoria's Secret. And during one very special night Camille had slid into that very outfit of Howard's fantasy. The uniform fit perfectly, and (true to his erotic reveries) white cotton panties had replaced Camille's usual silken undergarments. She protested Howard's purposely fumbling advances through giggles, as any good young Catholic girl should, although the woman who wore that outfit on that night had been seven years clear of those Sisters of Mercy.

Afterwards she had joked, "What would Jesus say?"

"I believe the man would have given me a high five," Howard answered. "Sister Agnes, however, probably would have put your shapely ass in a sling."

They both laughed. Soon after, they married. Cue Celine Dion's number and roll the closing credits. The End. Time to exit the theater all warm and fuzzy.

But not quite. The real end came a few years later

The grains shifted inside the twin spheres and most of them were gone from the upper portion. Howard sat transfixed, remembering how his love for Camille had somehow evaporated. Or maybe it had merely passed through time's hourglass to become something else, sifted to a fine dust that easily blows away.

Yes, their love had become something else, but what?

Watching the shifting grains dribble beneath Cupid's bow, Howard remembered another fantasy from those subsequent less-than-golden days.

Howard straps his wife to their bed and works over her naked flesh with the nub of a lit cigar. She screams while he laughs, shoving the entire Havana stogie down her gullet. From nowhere he produces a lit stick of explosives sputtering flame like a Fourth of July cracker. This he also rams into her mouth and waits for the woman's brains to explode and fill the sky with crimson goo, creating his own personal Independence Day, his unique fantasy payback.

"Cheating whore! Miserable spoiled cunt!"

"Lying bastard! Go screw another secretary!"

The searing of Camille's flesh remained only a fantasy. But the accusatory words, those were very real. With a delicious irony that their respective lawyers found both amusing and profitable, few of the couple's aspersions proved inaccurate. Time, that notorious indian giver, had reclaimed whatever love once had existed between them. From behind a polished mahogany table Martin Shengold from the legal firm of Matkoff and Shengold had a term at the ready for the couple's shared misery.

"Irreconcilable differences. It's an all-encompassing description, Mr. Jamison, legalese, if you will," the attorney announced alongside an expressionless Camille.

Howard could have sworn he saw blood dripping from the man's teeth.

"Alienation of affections would also suffice, but that sounds a bit harsh, don't you agree?"

At one hundred and fifty dollars an hour Howard agreed, silently nodding like a moron. He also would have agreed with the suggestion this man swing from the ceiling fan by his testicles.

"How much will these irreconcilable differences be costing me, Mr. Shengold?"

The man offered a smile and jotted a figure on his note pad, slipped the paper across the table. Somehow Howard managed not to laugh out loud.

"You feel like adding a vital organ or two with that request?"

No smile from Camille's attorney this time. "It's a fair figure, Mr. Jamison. I mean, considering the circumstances."

Howard turned to his lawyer. Attorney Michael Broder offered no words of comfort.

"The courts usually favor the wife," he told Howard. "It's the system. We can walk, of course, but these things tend to drag on and it will probably come to the same thing later. Your wife's terms are not uncommon. It could be worse."

"Yes, she could have asked to have my gonads made into earrings."

"You can keep the dog," Camille added. "For when Emma visits. She loves little Beeber, you know." She smiled broadly, turned to Shengold. "Our Emma just loves that Beeber."

Smiles from the two attorneys. It would have made a nice Rockwell painting had the late artist shown an interest in painting human snakes.

Howard hated the dog, an obnoxious toy poodle who barked incessantly at him. More than once the little fucker had pissed into his shoe. Camille hated the mean tempered canine too, so here was another "Gotcha!" for her. But Howard had no fight left in him.

On a grey December morning, ten years of marriage would dissolve with the stroke of a pen. House, car, even custody of his own child – Poof! these all would be gone, like those grains of sand that passed through that cheap hourglass. Cupid's golden arrows may have once hit their mark, but Howard knew their long lasting effect had been two dysfunctional hearts left to bleed out over this polished mahogany table.

"I want my hourglass," he had insisted, not even sure he knew why. He felt a great pit had opened, swallowing everything he had owned, and he just needed something – anything – he could point to and say, "Yes, this still belongs to me!"

There was the chance Camille would fight him for the timepiece simply because she could, but as it turned out she had no problem with the request. She leaned towards him, whispered so only he could hear. "It's yours. Because if you didn't take that piece of shit, I would have put in the trash."

Howard would not have admitted it to anyone who asked, but at that moment he realized why he loved that damned timepiece as much as he did.

He loved it because Camille hated it.

He stood up, turned to Camille and Shengold. "About these papers, I'll get back to you, okay? Fuck you very much."

And he walked.

The grains shifted more quickly through the glass now, and wasn't there something poetic in that? The less time that remained, the faster those grains seemed to pass through the hourglass' aperture.

The bottom portion had filled almost completely, but enough time remained for one last memory.

The phone call...

It had awakened him at the ungodly hour of - what had the digital clock read? – 2:37 a.m. For some reason he remembered that.

"Is this Howard Jamison?"

"Who – Who am I speaking to –?"

The caller ignored his question.

"Your wife is Mrs. Camille Jamison?"

"My ex wife. Or soon to be. We're separated. She and my daughter are staying at her sister's in Glenn Echoes. What is this abou...?"

"Mr. Jamison, my name is Officer John Tandy. I'm afraid there's been an accident involving your ... involving Camille Jamison."

The rest became a blur of policespeak gibberish, but the details that Howard managed to understand shook him awake.

"Car accident on the Interstate ... your wife ... so sorry ... need you to come to County General to identify the remains ..."

The woman on the slab inside the morgue was Camille, all right. Apparently she had been drinking, having come from Moxie's, a local hot spot for cheaters and the newly divorced. Her Honda had swerved into the oncoming lane of the Interstate and into the path of an eighteen wheeler hauling Jersey produce, whose shaken driver was full of unnecessary apologies.

Camille never stood a chance. One look at her ruined face told that story. For one horrific moment Howard thought it resembled an overripe tomato that had burst open.

Deep shame glutted his thoughts. Among Howard's recent fantasies, one had involved cutting her Honda's brake line. Pissed off to his limits he had almost done it, too, weeks earlier during another of his own benders. But he had remembered little Emma and decided maybe the alcohol was doing his thinking. Still, Howard could have sworn that fucking Beeber looked at him kind of funny that night as if he knew, and the mutt spent hours growling his displeasure deep inside his throat. Howard kept him locked inside the bathroom all night to avoid looking at him.

Camille's unforeseen death brought with it a myriad of decisions. The divorce papers had not yet been signed and he remained her legal husband, so those decisions fell on him. Howard decided on a simple funeral but no burial. Some family, some friends, a somewhat forced eulogy.

"She was my wife, the mother of my child. I loved her. I'll miss her." Short. Simple. And except for the wife and mother part, essentially bullshit. With a phone call to the crematorium and the selection of an ornate urn – the marmalade colored 'golden sunset' model – it was over.

But not quite.

Howard wanted to be there to see, and he was careful to select the last dress Camille Dorsey Jamison would ever wear. Asked to remove anything noncombustible, he noticed she had not been wearing her wedding band although he still wore his because it never occurred to him to take it off. He removed a necklace that had belonged to her grandmother, placing it into a plastic baggie with some of her other jewelry to dispense to Camille's sister. None of this thoughtfulness lessened the intense stare Howard received from the bald headed man at the cremation chamber who ran the show.

"You're certain this is what you want?" he asked, straightening Camille's blouse for her 1800 degree Fahrenheit trip into the next life. "Usually we don't dress them – especially not like this."

"It's something personal between my wife and me," Howard told him, deciding it would not be tasteful to ask if they had dressed her in the white panties he had left with the mortician. The bald man wiped his forehead and took one last look at the young woman dressed in her Catholic Girls' School uniform. He looked like he might smile but covered his mouth before it showed.

Yeah, he probably knew about the panties, Howard figured. He handed the man the golden urn and stayed to watch Camille's pinewood casket slip into a tunnel of flames.

The rest was ritual-by-the-book, a call from Edwin Fleuhr at the funeral home to come and collect the urn that now contained Camille's ashes, the requisite expressions of sympathy from the mortician and his comment about the tasteful selection of the vessel Howard had made for his wife's remains, then home to place the urn upon his mantel for friends and family to see. Howard could not resist a peek inside the urn. Its contents had been sifted thoroughly into a fine grain-like powder, and like the container that held them, Camille's ashes were as golden as the sun except for a few flecks of green he figured were the remains of her Our Sisters of Mercy uniform.

"Beautiful," he found himself saying aloud. It seemed a shame to hide her ashes inside a container where he could not always see them. Considering this, Howard saw no reason why he had to.

###

Beeber was in growling mode again. His eyes shifted from Howard to the hourglass and back. His growls grew deeper.

The grains had run out of the top portion of the glass, some of the powdery substance clinging to the sides. Time had come to flip the thing over, to start the whole process again. Howard turned the timepiece on its end. The winged Cupid was supposed to shift his position and turn over also, but the stupid cherub remained hugging the glass upside down. Maybe there was some meaning to be found in that image of Cupid with his bow, ridiculously hanging on to the timepiece like some kind of wounded bird.

The image was something to consider as Howard watched the object his late wife truly despised, watched the golden ashes (with flecks of green) again sift through the thin aperture inside his hourglass.

Howard had to smile. He could watch the shifting grains all day. And maybe he would.

Beeber's growls did not stop.

About the author

Kenneth Goldman, former English and Film Studies teacher, lives in Pennsylvania. His stories received seven honorable mentions in The Year's Best Fanatsy & Horror and appear in over 750 publications in the U.S., Canada, the UK, and Australia. He has written five books, *You Had me At ARRGH!!, Desiree, Donny Doesn't Live Here Anymore, Star-Crossed,* and *Of a Feather.*

~~ © 2015 Hourglass/Kenneth Goldman

BIZARRE TALES OF HORROR

Lowercase "G"
But Still Worth Keeping an Eye On

Edward Martin III

Michelle never really understood where all the blood was coming from.

It had to be coming from somewhere — blood doesn't simply appear.

At first it was all normal, or reasonable, circumstances.

The blood in the alley was probably left over from a fight or maybe someone hit a cat. Living in a big city comes with a lot of strange hazards, she reasoned. You have to learn to ignore the ones that don't directly affect you.

The blood outside her office probably belonged to the bum that sat out on the curb singing every morning. He didn't have a bad voice but he was a little annoying.

Someone could have shivved him for picking the wrong key. Again, this is something that can sometimes happen in the city. Tragic and sad, but true, like most things when you press so many people so densely together.

Even the drops on her kitchen floor could be explained. Maybe she had a nosebleed in the middle of the night and forgot about it. That can happen when you wander around in the middle of the night half-asleep. You stop noticing things, especially if you've had a stressful day. You just clean it up and move on with your life.

But lately, it was getting harder to explain. There's only so many different ways random blood can appear in your life before even the most reasonable explanation seems to pale in comparison to the fact that random blood is appearing in your life.

One afternoon, she ate lunch in the mall food court. The place was packed, but no one sat across from her the entire forty-five minutes she ate — unheard of!

When she stood up, she saw the puddles of blood on the bench, and the floor leading up to it. No wonder.

About half of the carpeted floor of the elevator she normally took was soaked in blood by the time she returned to work, so she stepped delicately over the puddle and took the stairs instead.

The first landing looked as if someone had spilled several pints, all in neat round puddles, and all fresh.

She stepped around it and continued up the stairs.

There was less blood on the next landing than the lower one, but still, the fact that there were fresh puddles of blood unnerved her even more.

By the fourth floor, she was still seeing blood, and sometimes on the stairs.

If she had been told by a friend that this was happening to the friend, her conclusion would have been immediate, and probably accurate. She realized this as she crested the sixth floor to a now-expected collection of puddles.

She stopped walking, leaned against the wall, crossed her arms, and said "Whoever you are, you can stop doing this right now."

Her voice echoed in the stairwell. There was no other response.

"I'm serious," she said. "This stalker shit's stopping right now."

She drew out her phone, and shook her head slightly when she saw the tiny circle-slash over the signal annunciator. "Of course," she muttered. She dropped it back into her purse.

"Do you hear me?" she called out.

Still nothing but her own echoes.

Slowly, she walked up one more flight.

On the landing was a puddle of blood.

She crouched near it.

She touched it with a fingertip. Part of her brain said "Stop that — that's evidence!" and another part of her brain replied "Evidence of what?" She chose to let both parts duke it out while she kept doing what she was doing.

It felt like blood.

She smelled it.

It smelled like blood. In fact, it smelled like fresh blood. Warm and metallic and homey.

She suddenly stopped thinking, and ran that one back. Had she really used the word "homey" to describe the smell of blood? She shook her head. She had indeed. How odd.

In her purse, she found a little baggie of tissues. Her emergency stash, for when allergy season surprised her.

Blood on your finger wasn't technically an allergy-related emergency. "But it still counts," she muttered to herself, as she wiped the blood from her finger.

She rolled the bloody tissue into a ball, wrapped a clean tissue around that, and tucked them into the purse pocket she always called the Useless Pocket. The Useless Pocket was a bit larger than a quarter, and could reasonably hold nothing that she knew of, until now.

Daintily, she stepped over the puddle, and continued climbing the stairs, avoiding any more puddles until she arrived at her floor.

She was late due to the stair adventure and because of this, it wasn't until nearly lunch when she suddenly noticed her hands.

"Gross!" she said, as she realized she needed to wash them.

Why it hadn't occurred to her until just now was crazy, but now that she thought of it, she had to. After all, she had touched someone's blood. Who knew what kind of horrible stuff was in it. Blood is filled with all of humanity's greatest evils, she reflected, as she stepped into the kitchen.

As the water ran, she stared at her fingers. She looked at all sides and all angles. There was no trace of blood. None at all. Now, to be fair, she hadn't exactly dipped her whole hand in there, but she expected to see something. She squinted, looking close at her fingerprints.

"There should be something there," she muttered. Her finger offered no answer.

So, she washed her hands anyway and ate a sandwich out of the vending machine. It was going to be a long and tiring day.

It was, in fact, longer and more tiring than she expected. Only as the Autumn sun was dropping out of sight across the factory-speckled horizon did she finally finish enough work to head home.

She leaned back in her chair for a moment's rest before gathering up her kit. It was then that she heard the singing.

Well, it wasn't exactly singing. It was more like keening, or wailing. Not horrible sounding, but tiny and thin.

She sat very still and listened. She couldn't quite catch words, but it seemed as if she almost could, as if there were words, but those words were just barely out of the range of what she could understand. She did understand the emotion behind it.

It was joy.

A strange sort of joy, though, and she could tell that by the way the notes would circle around each other. It was an animal joy, a pure joy. It sounded like the kind of joy you might associate with a dog greeting its owner, or a cat being petted until it purred. It was a contented joy.

She smiled, listening to it, in spite of her exhaustion of the day.

Then it struck her — where was it coming from?

She turned her head to get a bearing. It was close. She stood up, stepped away from her desk, and the sound grew dim. She stepped back and she could hear it better.

A nearby cubicle? No. Someone's computer? No. Under the desk?

She dropped to all fours and heard it much more clearly.

How strange — there was nothing under her desk.

Except for her purse.

She pulled it toward her. As her hand touched it, the song warbled a little, as if jumping to a higher level of joy.

She let the purse go, and the song calmed back down.

She opened the purse and dumped everything out onto the floor.

"Okay," she said. "Weird, but funny. Where's the pager?"

She sifted through the pile of things, all debris from her purse, and there was no pager, no extra musical device. It was what she had always carried in her purse.

Then she listened more carefully. Whatever it was, it was still in the purse.

She upended it and shook it, but nothing changed. She looked inside, and it was empty.

Almost.

The Useless Pocket, true to its name, had a tiny one-inch long zipper, which she had zipped closed this morning. She unzipped it and the music grew louder.

Stunned, she pulled out the tightly wrapped piece of tissue. It felt warm and soft.

She listened. The music was coming from the tissue.

Michelle cleared an area of the floor and set the tissue ball down. Slowly, she peeled it open. Inside was the other tissue, the one she had used to wipe the blood from her fingers. She gasped softly. The blood on the tissue was still wet, as wet as it had been when she touched it.

And it sang.

The blood sang to her.

She looked into it and it looked into her and it sang a song of joy.

On its wet surface, tiny golden speckles flickered and waved, reflecting the light.

She reached out and in the gentlest way possible, touched the edge of the tissue.

The blood separated from the tissue, liquid and beautiful, and formed a tiny droplet-pseudo-pod. It touched her extended fingertip, with equal gentleness.

The touch warmed her. The touch sent through her fingers a feeling entirely unlike any other feeling she had ever experienced. It felt good. Very good.

She curled a finger around the extended drop-let, and, like some shapeless sea creature, it curled around the finger in response, leaving the tissue.

She brought her finger close to her face to see this amazing thing.

Where it touched her, it felt wonderful, but she could not understand why. It flowed gently around her finger and over her hand as she watched. When it reached her palm, it gathered itself up, a tiny maroon pillar on the palm of her hand. It watched her as much as she watched it. There was no face on that shimmering surface, but she knew it was watching her. Waiting, or maybe making itself ready.

And then it sank in.

It sank directly into the skin of her palm. It didn't spread out. It didn't damage the skin at all. It was as if her skin suddenly absorbed it the way a towel absorbs water. There was no remnant, no markings, no indication at all.

Except for the feeling.

Michelle felt something amazing rush from her hand, up her arm. It rushed from her arm through her chest. It rushed through her whole body. That tiny drop of blood sang inside her and through her, and she finally understood the words and understood what it was doing to her.

It was worshiping her.

She felt its love for her. It was a simple pure love, an ecstatic love, the kind of love that could only come from the clarity of the devout, from someone — something — that has finally found its god.

It all unfolded for her.

She knew who she was. She knew what she was. And she knew why the blood was appearing, why it was following her, and why it wanted to be a part of her.

She also knew she wanted it, too. This was why she existed, why she walked the Earth, why she was here.

The blood needed her as much as she needed it. This was and had always been the way of things.

She stood, still in some shock from her realization, and then remembered the blood on the stairs. The lonely, lonely blood that tried to reach her, tried to find her, but she hadn't been ready yet to hear, she hadn't been ready yet to be the god it needed.

She smiled.

She was ready now.

"Hey, ma'am!" The voice distracted her. One of the night security crew approached her. "Are you okay? Are you supposed to be here this late?" he asked.

She looked at him, and her new eyes saw what was real.

Inside the vessel, she heard the blood singing to her, calling out to her.

"Let us come to you!" it cried in all its voices. "Let us join you," it begged.

She stepped out, reached toward the vessel, touched it, and made the blood welcome.

"Come to me," she whispered, but it was hardly necessary to speak — the blood knew her heart.

In less than a second, it leaped from its vessel and into her. She felt its strength, felt its purity, felt its song.

She hummed as she stepped over the empty vessel. She hummed a song she made up on the spot. A song without words, but richly filled with feelings and desires. She hummed a song of wonderment and freedom.

And then she went forth into the world to make it happen.

About the author

Edward Martin III is a writer and filmmaker scrabbling together a semblance of home in the Pacific Northwest. He's surrounded by looming evergreens with sullen boughs, mountains that ponder the nature of death, and a relentless sea that dissolves everything it touches. Also, there's a cat, primarily to offset all that rich delicious goodness. Edward's first novel "Through the Night" is being adapted to a feature film, and he is currently in production on several new films. His two most recent movies are "The Dream-Quest of Unknown Kadath" (an animated adaptation of the Lovecraft novel) and "Flesh of my Flesh" (a bizarre zombie horror set in the too-near future). Find him online at HellbenderMedia.com.

BIZARRE TALES OF HORROR

SHOCK TROOPS

Edward Martin III

Specialist First Class Vann was a soldier, but he was not a fighter. Certainly he had fought his way through Basic, like everyone else, but it was a hurdle he had to jump — not a means to an end. He wasn't a master at combat, an action hero, or even secretly a ninja. He was a Specialist First Class, and more specifically, a journalist.

He was not prepared for this madness. He was not prepared for the horrors he had witnessed, the terror he had experienced. It was nothing like what he and thousands of other soldiers trained to face. It was like nothing on this earth.

So, he did the only thing he could do, the only thing that made any sort of sense in the complete chaos of the battlefield.

He ran.

This was one thing he had been able to do well ever since he was a kid. He could run. He ran track in school, and set school records. He raced in training and his teams always won. He was the fastest man in his squad, the fastest man on the base.

But speed isn't a bonus in modern warfare with computer-tracked weaponry and sophisticated sensor technology. A hundred years ago, Vann would have been a scout, but his technology meant nothing now, and so he was a journalist.

But now the running mattered, oh yes, it mattered very much. Now Vann ran for his life while some sort of horror pursued him.

Some sort of horror that stood more than eight feet tall, was purple and black, screamed in a way that split the sky, and had killed three men in his squad before they ever knew there was an enemy in their midst.

Some sort of horror that had spikes and a whip tail and claws and teeth that weren't so much sharp as they were translucent needles, streaked bright red. It was a horror and no man faced with such a horror would not consider running, unless he were an idiot or a liar.

So Vann ran.

He ran until his lungs burned, he ran until his legs wobbled, he ran until he could run no more. Still, he continued running.

Behind him, he heard the thing following, loping along behind, panting like a dog, but always just behind him, always not quite able to reach him. He ran across an open field, knowing it was behind him, knowing its teeth and claws were stained with the rest of his squad.

He ran, knowing that such a thing could probably have caught up in half a dozen steps, but didn't He ran knowing that it was playing with him.

The buildings loomed out of the darkness, houses long abandoned, crumbling walls, debris and rubble everywhere.

For a moment, he allowed himself to hope this might help. He angled into the debris, between buildings, and into the light fog that covered everything.

His breath burned his throat and his heart hammered at his chest, and he knew that at this speed, he could only hope there wouldn't be any surprises ahead because he would probably plow full-speed into them.

The thing behind him cried out, and it chilled him hearing it. He ducked sideways between a couple of buildings, made another fast turn, and found himself in a small courtyard.

He paused, panting as quietly as he could. Maybe he'd lost it.

He tried to catch his breath as quietly as possible, hoping his heart wasn't as loud outside as it was inside.

Hope rested on one hand but on the other, he knew it wasn't going to last. He knew that his respite was at best short-lived. Still trying to be as quiet as possible, still trying to control his breathing and keep it quiet, too, he unholstered his pistol and stepped out from behind a building.

It wasn't until he was already flying through the air that he realized he'd been hit. The thing must have been mid-leap and collided with him, because nothing could have attacked that fast, he was sure of it.

Something seemed to punch against his arm three times, there was flashing and he wondered, for a fraction of a second, why he hadn't hit the ground yet. Then he did, and he was rolling and tumbling away from that monstrosity.

He jumped to his feet, turning, gun out. His hand was sore and he looked down, and realizing he had fired his weapon. Smoke curled from the muzzle. He spent an entire second praising his DI for getting those reflexes up and then turned back to the thing on the ground.

It lay writhing, eight feet from him, brown and black fluids pulsing out from the gaping impact holes.

Teeth snapped, but it could not move its head. Claws grasped, but it could not move its arms. The tail started moving, but then stopped. While he watched, the horror died.

He knelt before it. Raised his pistol once more.

"Might not want to do that," a voice behind him husked.

He spun.

She stood above him and it was only then that he realized both he and the creature had fallen into an old shallow foundation. She jumped down the four feet and stood with her rifle and eyes trained on the creature. Shaken, he saluted. "Sergeant, I think it's dead. I think I killed it."

She nodded. "I think you did, too," she said, "but I think you'd best be saving rounds anyway."

She watched it for a couple more seconds, and then seemed satisfied it was dead. Then she turned her rifle to Vann. "Are you bit?" she asked.

"What?" he asked, confused.

"Are you bit? Or scratched? Did it break your skin at all?"

The muzzle never wavered.

"I... uh, I don't think so," he said, but no sooner were the words out of his mouth than he noticed the itching. His left forearm started itching. Oh sure, he thought, just what I need to be doing right now when I want to be not moving is to have an itch.

The itch spread.

"Be sure," she said, "because I see your hand twitching."

"I got an itch."

"Scratch it."

He scratched, but it only got worse.

The itch became a burn and he kept scratching.

"Look at your arm," she said, and he wasted no time pulling his sleeve back.

A long thin scratch, hardly worth noting, ran from his elbow to the outside of his wrist. It was swollen and red.

He scratched it furiously. "Goddammit," he muttered, "itches like a sunnuvabitch."

"Yep," she said. "Sorry."

She raised her rifle.

"Wait! What the fuck, Sergeant!?"

"It scratched you. You know what happens next."

The burn had settled deeper, and instead of scratching, he was rubbing and squeezing his arm.

"I scratch back is what happens next. Look, it's almost gone. What the — why are you pointing your weapon at me?"

She looked puzzled, but the rifle never wavered. "You really don't know?" she asked.

"Don't know what?"

Now she was intrigued. "You haven't had the dreams?" she asked.

Vann shook his head. "I don't dream," he told her. "Not since –"

The twist in his guts was ferocious, like being punched by ten different guys, none of whom was happy. As he fell, a second explosion of pain went nova behind his eyes, a flare in his skull. He might have screamed.

A few seconds later, he became aware of her standing there, still a couple yards away, still watching him, rifle still aimed at him.

"Never met anyone didn't dream," she said. "How do you get that?"

Panting, he whispered.

"What?" she asked. "I can't hear you."

"I have a plate in my head," he growled. "Ever since I was twelve. I don't dream."

"That's cool," she said, nodding. "I guess that's a mixed blessing for you then because you don't know what's happening. You haven't had the dreams."

She peered at his uniform.

"Vann," she asked, "what do you know about our enemy?"

He shook his head. There was another blast of pain behind his eyes and he felt a twisting inside, impossibly inside. He fell back to his hands and knees.

"You see that thing on the ground behind you?" she asked. He didn't turn, but gagged, his throat twisting.More bolts of pain shot through his head. In between the increasing waves, he could still hear her.

"I've been hunting him for almost a day now," she said. "He and ten others. It's what happens when you fight a god."

At this, Vann looked up, scowling.

"Oh, not with a capital 'G'," she said. "I'm not sure exactly where He is, anyway. No, this is more like your average run-of-the-mill god. A smaller god. One that can't just wave its hand or whatever it has that looks like a hand and make things happen. It needs troops. Ground troops. And that's one of them."

She leaned down.

"You're looking at the only one in my squad that didn't get bit. Didn't get scratched. Over there," she nodded, "...was the first. He got away. I was hoping to stop him before he infected anyone else, but I suck, and now I'm sorry to say that you are also on the shock troops training fast-track for our sleeping god."

"What?!"

Vann tried to talk, but his guts clenched, his head felt like someone was going at it with a pick-axe, and he vomited.

Vomited something — not just food.

It shined in the darkness.

"That's something you won't need for your new life," the Sergeant observed. "I think it's a lymph node, hard to say."

Vann's mind slipped.

Wrenched.

"But this non-dreaming thing is pretty weird," she said. "That's how he controls you, through the waking dream he puts you in. We can sense it because we can also dream, but it's nothing to his dreams. His dreams shatter worlds. But if you don't dream then he can't see you."

Vann's hands and arms deepened in color to violet. He took a quick glance behind him at the corpse. He knew that color. His nails fell off as sharper claws pushed through his fingertips, even as the skin was hardening and darkening. It hurt, it hurt, oh Christ it hurt!

In his head again, a screeching, twisting pain that blew al the rest away. His mind tried to shut down but it wasn't happening. He couldn't stop feeling this, couldn't stop the pain, the pushing.

He gagged and coughed and gagged again. A spike ran through his head and he screamed and retched and something else pushed its way out. First his teeth – now useless – fell to the ground and then it clattered down with them, trailing stringy mucous and blood vessels.

The Sergeant leaned forward, squinting. "Wow," she said, "I guess we know who won that contest."

One part of Vann's mind marveled.

He'd always expected a surgical plate to look like a sheet of metal, but this looked more like a little piece of corrugated mesh, and small. Very small, maybe one by three centimeters.

The other part of his mind, however, was busy. It was dreaming.

Dreams flooded his mind, images from a distant past, pushing everything else away, even the pain.

In his dreams, he watched the history of the world unfold, the history he never knew existed, the history no man could ever have guessed.

In his dream, the Earth was still new and young.

It was the time of flames and chaos, ages before mankind, ages before there was life on the planet.

In this time, he saw the Beasts come to Earth. He saw them leaping and playing in the primordial lava, their bodies obscene and wondrous, their eyes burning like suns.

Then he saw the coming of the Scientists, beings nearly as old as the Beasts and nearly as powerful. Vann saw their crystal ships fill the skies and their beams of black dimensionless light slice the Beasts, one by one, into heaving, steaming corpses.

Then the Scientists left, but one Beast remained. Mutilated, crippled, and insane. It dragged itself into a cave, slid deep into the virgin Earth, and fell into a sleep of great power and great madness.

Vann saw all this in the blink of an eye, the flash of a thought, and then he was back in the ruined foundation.

The Sergeant shook her head. "Sucks," she said. "Not even our fight, but we still have to deal with the goddamn shellshock."

There was another twist and Vann felt everything shift. He screamed in pain, but halfway through, that pain turned to rage, to burning eternal fury. He looked up at the Sergeant through whirling violet eyes, and this time, she glowed brilliantly in the dark. Her scent was thick and heavy and meaty in his nostrils. He inhaled it and knew what must happen. She had to join them. She had to be changed and had to share the Sleeper's dream. They all had to join and grow in the brilliance of his new god. When the whole planet was ready, when all were of the same Dream, then they had to look outward, had to move outward, stretching across the solar system, across the galaxy, across the Universe. All had to share the Dream, to know the pain and suffering the Scientists had created. And then, maybe, somewhere in those journeys, they might actually find the Scientists themselves, and then—

"Sorry," said the Sergeant, raising her rifle. "I know what you're thinking. Not on my watch, no."

She squeezed the trigger and Vann stopped dreaming.

About the author

Edward Martin III is a writer and filmmaker scrabbling together a semblance of home in the Pacific Northwest. He's surrounded by looming evergreens with sullen boughs, mountains that ponder the nature of death, and a relentless sea that dissolves everything it touches. Also, there's a cat, primarily to offset all that rich delicious goodness. Edward's first novel "Through the Night" is being adapted to a feature film, and he is currently in production on several new films. His two most recent movies are "The Dream-Quest of Unknown Kadath" (an animated adaptation of the Lovecraft novel) and "Flesh of my Flesh" (a bizarre zombie horror set in the too-near future). Find him online at HellbenderMedia.com.

~~ © 2015 Shock Troops / Edward Martin III

SIMPLE

Brian D. Mazur

The elevator ground to a stop.

Scary sound that grind.

Always gave Liam pause.

Sounded like the gears guiding it were about to shatter.

Grimy doors slid open.

A young woman stood alone in the tomb-like interior.

New girl, he thought.

Her hair was short, black, and spiked in all directions.

Black eye shadow.

Black lipstick.

Pale face.

Black spiked collar.

Black short t-shirt showed a pale belly.

Black hip jeans and boots.

Tattoos inked both her arms ...

...and partially up her neck.

Piercings along both ears...

...nose ring...

...lip ring.

"Hi," he said to her as he stepped in.

She responded with only a quick flick of her gaze, and then her attention was to the numbers above the closing doors.

The girl gave off a dark vibe.

Only one light worked in the elevator.

Been that way for the three years he lived there.

Today it seemed darker.

It gave the little room that doomed feel.

As if, the shadows were crawling over his skin.

Moreover, they were cold.

He closed his eyes and calmed his insides.

This was strange.

When he opened them, they were at the ground floor and the doors slid open.

He let her step off first.

Outside the apartment, he went in one direction...

...she in the other.

"Have a good day," he said just before the parting.

She just kept walking.

Liam's day...

Work the morning shift at the Gilbert Coffee Café 3 blocks up Gilbert Avenue.

At 11:30, head to school for two classes.

5:00, back to work for the evening shift.

When he arrived home around nine o'clock, the usual crowd hung out front.

Liam said his hello's.

At the elevator the girl from the morning was waiting, her eyes glued to the descending numbers; arms crossed across her chest.

"Hi," Liam said.

Her response - a snapping of gum and continued chewing.

Beneath the Goth, he saw bumps hidden by white makeup.

Small, up turned nose, held diamond-like stud along the nostril.

Hazel eyes beneath heavy, black false eyelashes, stared unblinking up.

High cheekbones gave her a very model like look, which she might have been if taller.

Or not Goth.

Liam decided she was rather pretty.

The elevator arrived and they stepped on.

He let her go first again.

The ride up was silent of course.

Liam got off at his fifth floor.

"Have a good night," he said, stepping off.

Closing of the doors behind him was the only sound.

Liam's life had become a series of repetition.

Work.

School.

Work.

School.

All this he knew while planning the early part of his life.

After two weeks, the odd elevator girl became part of that routine.

Like a rolling snowball.

Hello to girl.

Silence returned.

Goodbye to girl.

Still silence.

Work.

School.

Work.

Hello to girl.

More silence.

Goodnight to girl.

Silence.

He talked to his co-worker Bryce about her...

...between orders of cappuccinos, frappuccinos, and coffees.

Bryce had long hair in a ponytail...

...a weak beard along his jaw.

He was skinny as a rail.

"I can't understand how someone can't respond to a simple hello. I mean, I'm not looking for deep conversation. A simple "Hi", that's it! Every day for fourteen days, twice a day . . . twenty-eight "Hi's" and twenty-eight "Have a nice day" or "Have a nice night". How can that be ignored?"

"Liam, man, you're missing something here."

Liam handed a customer a coffee.

"What?"

Bryce was wiping down the equipment with a gray rag.

"Well, think about it. Every day you get on the elevator she's on it. Every night you return home, there she is again."

"Yeah?"

"If she wanted to avoid you, she'd be taking the stairs. If you wanted to avoid her, you would take the stairs or either of you would change your routine. Leave five minutes earlier or later, either way."

Liam was silent.

"You suggest that we're doing this on purpose?"

With a raised eyebrow signifying a "you're finally catching on" look, Bryce pointed at him.

That night the number of people hanging on the front steps was down to seven.

However, at the elevator, she was there again.

At first, both kept up their part of "The Dance"

Silence.

The ride was more of the same.

The doors opened to the fifth floor.

Liam reached out and held the Open button.

Her eyes, a quick click toward him, and then her stare returned to the hallway stretched before her.

"Would it kill you to say hi when I say hi?" he asked, his voice steadier than he expected.

She didn't respond.

The tattoo on her right arm was a snake.

Black and yellow.

The single light room seemed to get darker.

The snake moved, coiling around her upper arm.

Liam stepped off the elevator.

He turned back to look at her.

As the doors slid shut, her gaze, though still straight ahead, didn't meet his.

In the next moment, quiet surrounded him.

It was disorienting.

The doors and walls are paper-thin.

There is always an assault of loud music, video games, or conversations.

When he first moved in, he didn't sleep much.

Overtime he grew accustomed to it.

Liam was uncomfortable, like he was being squeezed around his chest.

He hurried to his apartment.

"A trick of light and your imagination," Bryce offered.

It was his logical response to the tattoo snake's movement.

"Probably, but it still freaked me out."

"So you try again. Next time you be less aggressive in your approach. Introduce yourself first."

"Simple," Liam said, nodding.

That night, the number on the front steps was down to five.

"Where is everybody?" he asked no one in specific.

All heads turned toward him.

Young.

Old.

Fat.

Thin.

No one answered.

Liam maneuvered his way through the small crowd without touching anyone.

This was something, since not one tried to move out of his way.

At the elevator, she was there again.

This time he approached her with, "Hi my name is Liam."

The dirty doors slid open.

"I know your name," she said, stepping forward.

"How do you know?" he asked standing beside her.

"We haven't exchanged a word in three weeks."

The doors closed and the elevator jerked upward.

She watched the numbers climb.

He kept glancing at the snake on her arm.

It didn't move.

"Why haven't you said a word to me?'

The elevator reached the fifth floor.

This time she held the Open button.

Turning to him, he saw the tattoo on her left arm.

Another snake.

Red,

Yellow.

Black.

It started at the elbow, wrapped around her upper arm and disappeared under the sleeve of the black tee.

The black tipped head poked out on her neck, just below the spiked collar.

A smile slithered across her face.

The snakes' forked tongue licked at her white neck.

Liam stumbled back out of the elevator.

The next morning, Liam left his apartment five minutes earlier.

No scary girl on the elevator.

At night, he delayed his trip home by cleaning in every corner of the shop, which bought him an hour.

Bryce's latest suggestion occupied his thoughts as he walked home.

"You've been working and going to school seven days a week for two years. Now this chick has you obsessing. All that got you tired, maybe seeing things. Why don't you take a couple of days, I'll cover, could use the money anyway, and go see your brother upstate."

As he came up on his building, Liam stopped short.

This time, only three stood on the front steps.

Silent.

A chill prickled his neck.

"H-Hey, where is everyone tonight?"

The three heads rotated his way.

More silence.

Liam rolled his eyes and ascended the stairs past them.

"We don't know," one said.

Liam turned around.

He didn't know which one spoke.

One had long dirty blonde hair and beard. He was tall as he was round.

Number 2 had a buzz cut and a few days of growth on his jaw.

The third, black, wore a red-hoodie that shaded most of his face with the exception of large, white, emotional brown eyes.

He was the one that spoke.

"They're all gone, man." He stepped out from behind Buzz Cut "Others too."

"We ain't going back in," Dirty Blonde Hair said.

"What about all your stuff?" Liam asked.

"It's simple," Red Hoodie offered, "we're leaving it all."

Liam looked to the building's front door, his reflection murky on the black glass.

He looked like a dark ghost.

From behind...

...she appeared.

Greasy on the glass.

Eyeless.

Cold impeded on the warm spring night.

Liam closed his eyes.

When he opened them, it was only him once again.

He turned to see the trio heading up the street.

The building felt empty.

A glimmer of luck was with him though.

No sign of her anywhere.

He pushed the up button to call the elevator.

He found himself holding his breath as he watched the numbers descend...

...and the cable and gears cry, like a wailing ghost.

The doors slipped open...

...to an empty car.

Liam felt his shoulders relax.

He stepped off at the fifth floor and headed down the hall.

Halfway down, he stopped.

The building felt lifeless.

Each apartment he passed...silent.

The lighting in the hallway grew dim.

It was like looking through tea.

From behind him, the doors of the elevator opened.

The silence was broken by...

Chink...

...chink...

...chink...

Liam turned.

She approached him...

...as if she floated through the brown light.

She was dressed in a sleeveless black tee shirt and the now familiar white makeup.

Instead of jeans, she wore a black leather skirt and black stockings.

The sound was from the bracelets on both her wrists.

Chink…

…chink…

…chink…

He didn't move.

She stopped in front of him.

He kept a careful eye on those tattoos.

The snakes didn't move.

Gazing up at him with horrible, bottomless, dark eyes, she reached up to his face, gently ran the back of her hand down his cheek, and along his jaw.

Her touch was warm.

"Eve," she said. "My name is Eve."

He watched her mouth move as she talked, her lips a deep red, edged in black.

From the distance he heard himself force the question, "Why now?"

She touched a finger to his chest…

…and there she left it.

Despite her warmth, Liam felt cold.

Deep-in-the-soul cold.

He wanted to run to his apartment.

Lock the door.

Hide under the bed…

…or in the closet.

However, he could not move.

His gaze fell to her arms.

The snakes began to roil.

Black.

Yellow.

Black.

Yellow.

Red.

The snakes, tongues licking, bodies coiling…

…moved with greater enthusiasm.

"Why now?" she repeated.

God, he didn't want to know the answer.

He wished to go back…

…to be happy not knowing her.

Clicking her tongue against the roof of her mouth, she said, "Like all the others …"

Eve walked her index and middle fingers up his chest.

Liam tried to pull away.

"…it is simply your turn."

The snakes rose from her arms.

Heads twisting…

…thrusting.

Liam heard the elevator door slide open.

Out stepped Red Hoodie, Dirty Blonde, and Buzz Cut.

"Wrong floor," Dirty Blonde said.

"I knew comin' back was a bad idea," Red Hoodie added.

"We need our money and cards," Buzz Cut offered.

The doors slid closed behind them.

Buzz Cut frantically pushed the button.

The elevator didn't respond.

The three of them had Eve's attention.

She made a hissing sound, like a broom across concrete.

She pulled away from Liam.

Her attention now locked on the men.

With casual steps, Eve made her way to them.

Why not, they weren't going anywhere.

There was nowhere to go.

They began to shriek - clawing at the elevator doors in frantic desperation.

Finding his legs, Liam ran for his apartment, chased by the cries behind him.

He fumbled with the keys from his pocket.

The lights in the hall began to flicker.

The three men's screams filled the air.

Liam didn't look, forcing his concentration on getting in the apartment.

Then, he dropped the keys.

Hissing.

Hissing.

At the same time came a dramatic and sudden silence.

She was done with them.

That was bad news for Liam.

Chink!

Chink!

Hands shaking, he picked up his keys, lifting them by the one for the door.

Lock one…

Click!

Lock two…

Click!

Third…

Snap!

He was in.

There were the two deadbolts and the knob to lock.

Clack!

Clack!

Snap!

On the open counter, there sat a butcher block of knives.

His mother insisted he take them even though he didn't cook.

Thank, God, she did.

He ran for them.

Reaching…

"Now, where were we?"

Liam spun around...

Eve sauntered toward him.

Chink!

Chink!

Chink!

Those damn bracelets.

Again he could not move.

The snakes began to writhe, extending out in both directions.

Tongues licked the air between them.

Liam braced himself.

Eve looked him up and down with oily eyes.

"Liam," she sighed. "You simply can't escape your turn."

Before fear tore what remained of his sanity apart, he plunged the knife into her heart.

"Neither can you," he said, voice shaking.

Eve gasped, her eyes flared wide.

Liam saw himself in their inky depths.

Time slowed down.

The snakes writhed around him ...

Red.

Yellow.

Black.

Hissing in his ears...

...snapping at his face... tongues rippling with vengeful hunger.

Liam pushed the knife deeper.

A choking sound escaped her.

The serpents dipped and twisted.

He pulled the out the knife – it made a sucking sound.

Eve dropped to the floor.

The snakes collapsed to the floor on either side of her.

Dead.

She stared up at him.

The empty stare of death.

Liam dropped the knife.

He began to laugh.

It was over – whatever that was, was over.

Relief swept over him, he felt his face flush.

He grew dizzy with elation.

Laughter, his laughter, astounded him.

Then, he was gasping for breath.

There was pain in his wrist.

Hot.

Burning.

Pushing up his sleeve, he saw two swollen holes.

Pierce marks.

Snake bite.

Red.

Oozing a clear liquid.

One of them got him.

The room swam.

Liam fell to his knees.

Wheezing, he fell onto all fours.

Strings of drool ran from his mouth…

…puddling on the floor beneath him.

He collapsed.

His chest tightened.

Breath grew shorter.

As the room dimmed, he looked to her.

Her lifeless eyes locked on the ceiling.

As darkness ate at the edges of his vision, her head turned to him and she blinked.

Then one final cold shudder took him.

About the author

Brian D. Mazur's publishing credits include "Raven and the Darkness" in the 2009 Horror Bound anthology Return of the Raven, also in 2011 "What She Dreams" in another Horror Bound publication, Fear of the Dark. In 2012 my short story, "Home Coming", was published in Wicked East Press', Behind Locked Doors and the same year, from Jaletta Celgg & Frances Pauli, the anthology Wandering Weeds: Tale of Rabid Vegetation, a dark fantasy influenced, "Oh, Dark Tumbleweed" was published. Halloween of 2013 from Sekhmet Press, Wrapped in Red: 13 Tales of Vampiric Horror, my short, "Shattering Glass". Also released Halloween 2013, from Diabolic Publications, another vampire tale, "Dumaine", published in Dying to Live.

The last twenty years have seen numerous publications in smaller press magazines as well, including House of Pain, Outer Darkness, Graveworm Press, MindMares, and Mythic Circle.

~~ © 2015 Simple/Brian D. Mazur

SOUTH OF HEAVEN

Anthony Parker

Brandon eased his pickup truck down the long winding driveway, threw it into park and killed the engine. His mobile home sat before him illuminated in the immaculate glow of the full moon, the unfinished addition still reminding him of a long weekend ahead. But he knew that it would be worth it when it was complete.

The only concern he had was his bedroom window. The seal around it had rusted over the years and now only a make-shift awning covered it to keep the rain and any other precipitation out so the floor would not get wet. It would do for now but he knew it would not last forever.

He opened the cab door, stepped out into the warm summer night and turned his attention toward the yard where the big oaks stood, wondering if something might be hiding in the shadows of the giant trees sitting fifty yards from his house. Was that movement he saw or just a trick of the moon, slipping in and out of the low, thick clouds? He could almost hear their voices. We see you, Brandon.

He pulled his dirty cap off and wiped the sweat from his brow. "Everything looks in order," he thought and he made his way to the front door. He took a final look back, studying the scene that had never given such a sense of uneasiness before. The leaves danced in the slight breeze, singing a song of impending rain. Brandon looked up into the sky to see the moon disappear behind a wall of clouds like a well-timed magic trick.

A sudden roar in the sky made Brandon freeze in his tracks. Three helicopters flew overhead, keeping a straight formation as they made their way across the heavens. Watching as they disappeared into the dark skyline beyond the trees, his sense of uneasiness intensified before entering.

The keys clinked onto the coffee table as Brandon flicked on the light switch and kicked off his dirty work boots. Then he made a b-line for the kitchen. He pulled open the refrigerator door and stared into the barren appliance. The only thing left was some meatloaf and a case of beer, so he grabbed a cold one and the leftovers and slid his snack into the microwave. He chugged the first beer and grabbed another while the food rode in circles, like a merry-go-round for meals.

Brandon grabbed the plate, quickly released it and waved his meaty hands back and forth to cool the burning sensation. Eventually, he maneuvered it onto a tray and retreated to the living room. He plopped down on the couch and turned on his big fifty-five inch television. Surround sound speakers along with the 1080p high-definition made Brandon feel like a king in his rinky-dink home. Brandon ate, drank and laughed, oblivious to the brewing storm outside.

Startled by the loud clap of thunder, Brandon jerked from his slumber sending the remote flying across the room, the tray falling to the floor amid the crash of what-knots. He walked over to the lamp by the sofa, grabbed the chain and yanked it. Nothing. "Power must be out." Brandon mumbled to himself.

He lumbered towards the bedroom, pulling his t-shirt off. The cool pillow felt good against his sunburnt face as he fell face first onto the bed.

A lucid dream of childhood entered his mind as he slept. He was riding his bicycle down Main Street, on his way to indulge in one of Mrs. Roberson's famous apple pies. Always a favorite at the county fair. After he had sufficiently stuffed himself of the delicious treat, he hopped on his bike and rode home. On his way, a black and tan Doberman appeared out of nowhere, like a ninja, and gave chase. After reaching the front yard, Brandon jumped down from his bicycle and ran to the front door only to find it locked. He pounded and screamed at the top of his lungs, "Mom, please open the--"

THUMP! THUMP! THUMP!

Brandon jumped out of bed, heart pounding, and looked around the dark bedroom. He rubbed the sleep from his eyes. "Wow, that dream was--"

THUMP! THUMP!

A tiny, shrill voice cried from outside, "Please! Is anybody home?"

Lightning pierced the sky and the thunder boomed like two giants slugging it out. Brandon felt a cold chill race down his spine. Who could be out there at this time of the night? In this kind of weather? Brandon grabbed the wooden baseball bat that he kept by his bed and crept down the hallway toward the front door.

"Who's there?"

"Please, I need help. I'm being chased."

Brandon looked out of the peephole on the front door. A young girl Brandon guessed about sixteen years old stood with both of her hands clutched to her elbows like she was hugging herself to keep warm. She glanced over her shoulder every few seconds then turned back to the door and knocked again.

"Please, let me in." He could hear the hysteria in her voice about to break into tears.

Brandon unlocked the front door, pulled it back just enough to poke one of his blue eyes around the corner.

"What are you doing out at this time? Where are your parents?"

The young girl cried. "You don't understand. I barely got away. This is the first place I came to."

Brandon opened the door the rest of the way and revealed the wooden stick of justice. He flicked the latch on the screen door and pushed it open. The young girl ran inside. Brandon peeked out into the night to make sure nobody had followed her, went back inside and shut the door, satisfied nobody was out there.

Resting the bat up against the door he looked at the young girl standing by the couch, her clothes soaking wet. They stuck to her like a magnet. Brandon lit an oil lamp for her.

"The bathroom is down the hall, second door on the right. My sister comes over every now and again to do her laundry. I believe she may have left some of her clothes in there. You can put them on if you want."

Sobbing, she hung her head and mumbled, "Thanks."

Brandon sat in his recliner and leaned his head back on the soft, leathery headrest. What is she running from? Probably got into an argument with her parents or something. The young girl came out of the bathroom with the oil lamp, dressed in a pair of jogging pants and a plain white t-shirt that hugged her chubby figure.

"I found these in the closet with the towels. Are you sure your sister won't mind?"

Brandon shook his head. "I'm sure. It will be a day or two before she comes back here. So do you have a name?"

The girl looked down, twisting her big toe in the shaggy carpet like a child in trouble.

"Candace."

"I'm Brandon. So you want to tell me what's going on, Candace?"

She sat the lamp down on the table beside the couch and stared at the dancing flame in the clear cylinder.

"My mother came home from work today and was complaining about a new patient that had just been admitted. She said he was so unruly that he bit her on the arm. By the time she got home the blood was seeping through the bandages. It looked pretty rough. I went through my usual routine, a snack and homework before I fell asleep in my room. I woke up to father's agonizing screams. When I opened my door, I saw… I saw…"

A great ball of emotion had lodged itself in her throat. She tried to finish her thought but struggled. Brandon got up and offered her a seat on the recliner.

"Here you go, Sweetie."

Brandon walked into the kitchen, grabbed a glass from the cupboard and filled it with cool tap water. He handed it to Candace and took a seat on the couch beside the dancing flame.

"Thanks." Candace gulped the water down. Wiping a few tears from her face Candace continued. "When I opened my door, I saw my Mother sitting in the hallway covered in blood. I watched as her teeth sank into Dad's neck, ripping the flesh and snapping cartilage. The blood shot out from the wound and hit the wall, splattering all of the photos. I yelled at her to stop. She twisted her head in my direction and growled, pieces of dad hanging from her mouth. Her eyes were all red and glossy. Dark blue veins running down her neck. That's when I knew I wasn't looking at my mother anymore. So I ran."

Brandon sat on the edge of the couch, elbow resting on his knee, fingernails positioned in his mouth. He listened to the horror of Candace's nightmare. He couldn't believe what he was hearing and even had to wonder for a moment if he was still in his dream. "So your Mom is chasing you?"

Candace shook her head. "No."

"Then who is?"

"When I got outside, there were more of them like Mother roaming around in the yard. They had that weird look. Like they were very sick...or even dead. They saw me and ran after me. I felt like a rabbit being hunted."

Doubt began to creep into Brandon's thoughts, "You sure this isn't some nightmare you've had?"

"You think I would run two miles to knock on a stranger's door because of a bad dream? I wish it was just a dream!"

"Sorry. I just haven't heard anything like this before." Brandon stood up and grabbed his cell phone. "I have an idea. Why don't I call emergency services and have them come straighten this out?"

Candace exhaled with relief. "That would be great!"

Brandon dialed, put his phone to his ear and frowned.."That's odd."

"What?"

"It's playing an emergency broadcast in the background."

The wind howled outside, shaking the trailer like a tin can. The rain beat on the sides of the mobile home making it hard to think, much less talk. Before Candace could ask what it was saying, a thump was heard outside in the vicinity of Brandon's bedroom.

"Damn it! That's probably the awning. I've got to fix that or we'll have a river in here."

Brandon grabbed his raincoat and umbrella from the back of the door and headed out. "I'll be back in a couple of minutes."

Candace nodded and curled up in the recliner.

Brandon ran to his pickup and dug out his small flashlight, work hammer and nails. On his way to the end of the trailer he waded through ankle deep mud. It's getting bad out here.

The make-shift awning, a two foot wide by one foot long piece of sheet metal nailed to two fence posts, lay on the ground. Brandon grabbed one of the fence posts and pushed until it stood up, the other post mimicking the movement. A small puddle of water had started to form in the floor of the bedroom. Glad I got out here when I did. Brandon jogged back to the truck and grabbed his ladder. Placing the awning flush against the window frame he pulled out a couple of nails and drove them in, flashlight resting in his mouth. "There, that should do the…"

Brandon fell backwards into the mud as the thunder boomed, dropping his hammer and flashlight in the process. He could sense the increasing intensity of the storm and decided that he should get back inside.

Picking himself up Brandon stopped dead in his tracks. Through the low, soft gust of wind he could hear loud moans filling the air coming from the dark shadows of the oak trees bordering his land. Brandon stood motionless, straining to see into the dark of the forest, but the heavy rain refused him any vision.

The lightening flashed and in the clearing half-way to the tree line, an army of creatures marched in the heavy downpour. Brandon could not believe what he was seeing. He wanted to retrieve his flash-light but his legs simply would not move. A fear such as he'd never known gripped him into immobility. More and more of these ghastly creatures trudged and limped out of the woods like wounded soldiers returning from a war, clothes tattered and torn.

Aided by a steady display of brilliant flashes one of the creatures in particular caught Brandon's eye. It was Patricia Green, an old flame from high school. Patricia limped and moaned with the rest of the group, her jaw swinging open like a gate unhinged. Brandon's skin popped with goosebumps. Patricia Green had died in a car accident three days ago.

"What the hell is going on!"

The army of monsters stopped and let out a collective angry moan. They sniffed the air like a pack of hungry wolves, then locked their gaze on Brandon. The horde quickened its pace and, with arms extended, went straight for him.

Brandon freed his feet but they tangled with the rain, soaked grass, causing him to belly flop onto the ground. Wrestling with the mud, he finally got to his feet and made his way around to the front yard. He looked back at the pack and guessed that there were at least a couple dozen of them giving chase. Brandon made it to the front steps and grabbed the railing, pulling himself up onto the porch.

The horde was closing in on him.

Brandon twisted the knob. Locked! He remembered the dream he had with the dog chasing him, except this time it was a flock of the living dead and this was real.

Damn it! She locked it! Brandon pounded on the door. "Let me in!"

The door opened. Candace stood in the doorway and peeked outside. Her mouth dropped, "Oh my God! They've found me!"

Brandon ran inside, closed the door and barricaded himself against it. He could hear the pack nearing the porch. Within minutes the door began to shake. Fear hit Brandon like a runaway car. "They're trying to get in! Quick, go look out one of the back windows and see if any are out there."

"Okay."

Candace ran to the backdoor and peeked out the small umbrella shaped window. "Nothing," she reported and hurried back.

The door shook harder and harder.

"Okay, here's what we're going to do. I'm going to let go of the door. When I do, we make a break for the backdoor. When we're outside, head straight for my pickup and get in. It should be unlocked. We have got to get out of here!"

"Yeah, okay."

He could hear the terror in her voice and hoped she wouldn't let him down.

"Okay. On the count of three. Ready? One...two... three. GO!"

Brandon let go, grabbed his keys and took off like an Olympic sprinter. The door behind him burst open and the foul stench of death permeated the air like a sewer line busted, crashing over Brandon and Candace in waves. They fled out the back of the trailer choking on the horrid smell. The dead were too slow to catch them for now.

They ran back around to the front yard, unnoticed by the army of dead on the front porch, and jumped in the pickup truck. Brandon's hands shook while he fumbled the key into the ignition. On the first try it roared to life. Brandon threw the gear shift into reverse, and sped down the driveway backwards. The dead turned toward the noise of the truck and descended down the stairs.

The truck obeyed every command Brandon gave it, speeding down the dirt road like a race champ. Brandon's voice suggested the edge of hysteria. "So those are the things chasing you?"

"Yeah," said Candace, her voice small and shaken. "What are we going to do?"

Brandon scratched his head. "I think we need to go to the police and see if they can help us."

Relieved by the idea, Candace mumbled, "Okay. That sounds great."

No more than twenty minutes had passed when Brandon had to slam on his brakes. The truck lunged forward and almost hydroplaned before coming to a complete stop. They sat in the cab and stared at the massive car pile-up sitting in front of them.

"What happened here?" Brandon questioned. Then he remembered the three helicopters that had flown over his house. Could this be what they were responding to? He hoped this was just a small bump in the road on their way to finding help.

Brandon looked at a sign to his left, JAMESTOWN CITY LIMITS.

Candace began to cry. "Oh my God. What do we do now?"

Brandon looked up at the sky through his hazy windshield. The storm had let up and the clouds were beginning to break. "Looks like we're going to have to walk. There is no way I can drive around the wreckage. Shouldn't be more than a couple miles to the police station."

Candace shuddered, "You think it's safe? There might be more of those things out there."

Brandon rummaged through the endless supply of tools in the backseat of the cab and pulled out a rusty crowbar. "This might not be much but if one gets close just brain him real good with it, okay? If anything it should buy you some time. But try to stay close to me."

Candace began to weep, "I'm scared."

Brandon placed a hand on her shoulder. "Yeah, me too. We will find help though. I promise."

They stepped out into the damp night and walked around the wreckage. Cars sat sideways in the road with their windshields smashed while other cars were flipped over.

After a short while, the moon appeared from be-hind the dark fury that had covered the sky for most of the night. Its temporary glow lit the immediate path for Brandon and Candace but didn't reach quite far enough to illuminate the small army of walking dead headed their way.

About the author

Anthony Parker is a short story author and proud father of two. His work has been included in The Storyteller, December 2013 and a non-fiction piece in a company newsletter titled Spotlight. When he's not frightening his friends with his writing, he's most likely frightening his wife or mother. His short term goal is to have more short stories published within the year. His long term goal is to have a novel written by next year.

~~ © 2015 South of Heaven/Anthony Parker

BIZARRE TALES OF HORROR

THE COLLECTION

Anthony Parker

Detective Eric Turner got to the trailer park just as the police had marked off the crime scene. There was a growing crowd as he surfed his way through the throngs of people. Turner never understood why people were so interested in seeing a dead body. Must be some primitive instinct. The human condition.

Turner felt a sense of dread as he watched one of the officers run out of the home to the backside of the trailer and vomit. He never liked dealing with the messy ones.

Twenty years on the job could never prepare you for the unspeakable. Just when he thought he had seen it all, something more sinister reared its ugly head.

A man wearing oil-stained overalls came waddling towards the detective hesitantly. He was a behemoth of a man with his head hanging low against his hairy chest, chins jiggling with each step. He tried to form words, but he only stammered as he tried to speak. Finally, Turner cut him off. "Are you a relative?"

"No, sir. M' name's Stedam. I own this here trailer park."

Turner got out his notepad. "I need you to take me to the scene and tell me everything you know."

Stedam grew pale. "I weren't countin' on going back in there. Do I have to?"

"Yes, I'm afraid you do."

Stedam's cheeks began to bounce, fighting the urge to cry. He managed to control it and stepped in front of the detective.

"Right this way. I tell ya, I ain't never seen anything like this."

The screen door screeched in protest as the two walked inside. An overwhelming stench struck Turner's nostrils. It reminded him of the meat packing plant in town. They walked through the living room and into the kitchen before Stedam put a shaky hand against the table.

"I just can't go back there again. Please. You're gonna have to go by yourself. Last door on the right."

Turner grunted in disgust as he walked past Stedam and into the hallway. These trailer park owners charge an arm and a leg to rent one of these homes and then they don't bother with the upkeep.

The floors dry rot and people fall through, breaking a leg. Then if something even worse happens they can't...

Turner saw it.

A huge pentagram was painted in blood on the ragged floor. The curtains were drawn and candles lit in each corner of the room. Seated next to the bed were the dead bodies of three young girls, naked. Turner guessed them to be sixteen, maybe seventeen. The corpses had been cut open and sewn back shut. They had been wiped clean from head to toe. It struck Turner that they looked as if they had been killed, hollowed out and stuffed like big game trophies. He believed they called it taxidermy. Turner started to back out the room when he noticed the closet door was ajar. He stepped around the pentagram, doing his best to avoid the unholy nightmare on the floor. When he opened the door, Turner had to cover his mouth and fight the urge to gag. A gray and red pile of sludge sat on a large platter with a cup of dark red liquid. He was close enough to make out the shape of a human liver sitting on the plate.

Turner couldn't fight it anymore. He darted through the house and vomited just outside the screen door.

Wiping his mouth, he walked over to one of the officers, "Do we have a suspect yet?"

"Yes, sir. Suspect is in the back of the squad car."

Turner gathered himself and walked past the officer, walking to the car in big strides, his anger rising with each step. What he saw in the backseat froze him in his tracks.

A young girl, Turner guessed maybe seventeen, sat with her hands cuffed behind her, rocking back and forth. Her face and neck were covered in blood. It had matted in her hair and crusted on her clothes. Turner was fairly certain that most of the blood wasn't hers. He thought only a man with special skills could have done something like this. She had to have had an accomplice.

"Was she alone?"

"Yeah. She was sitting in the closet eating from a big platter. After each bite she would mumble something about her father. Couldn't make heads or tails of the rest of it."

Turner stared at the wide-eyed nightmare. She was eating from the platter? How could a once beautiful teenage girl do something so abhorrent? He rubbed his temples with thumb and index finger, the emergence of a headache forming in his head.

"Anyone get a hold of her father?"

The officer shifted his stance.

"No, sir. We haven't found any contact information and the girl won't talk."

"Okay. Go ahead and take her downtown and get her cleaned up. I'm going to try and talk to her to-morrow. I also want the rest of you guys to check fin-gerprints. I think she may have had an accomplice."

"Yes, sir."

Turner hopped into his car and left the trailer park, images of the three girls playing back in his mind as he drove. It was definitely one the more sinister crimes he had ever witnessed. But this one bore something dark. The pentagram was done in blood and that alone was evil. Something about the scene felt off, though. He thought about the candles and the odor they gave. At least he thought it was the candles. The room had a hint of sulfur to it and he couldn't figure out how candles would emit such an odor. He decided to drive home and try to rest before questioning the suspect. Turner wanted to do his best to forget about the images for the time being and there was no better remedy than the half bottle of liquor sitting on his nightstand.

Lucid nightmares filled his head as he slept, with visions of his late wife invading his sleep. She had only been dead for two years but it felt like an eter-nity. Even in death and dreams she remained as beautiful as the first time they had met. She wore a white gown soaked in blood and carried a small book, reciting a passage from it. Turner couldn't understand her incoherent murmuring. He tried to call out, but his throat clinched, offering a low garble. In a surprise move, she turned and met his gaze. Horror shot through him as her beauty was stripped away in an instant, her face taking the form of a mutilated corpse. Her eyes rolled back in her head as she gnashed her teeth at him. Then in a low growl she spoke. "They're coming for you." Cold sweat rolled from his head as he sat up from his nightmare. He didn't sleep well the rest of the night.

Turner sipped his coffee and watched the frenetic pace of the police station as officers darted all around, saving the world one call at a time. He pondered how he was going to get the girl to talk. According to the arresting officer, the only thing he had heard her mumble, since bringing her in, were the words "hungry," but when they brought her some food, she wouldn't eat.

Turner grimaced at the image his mind conjured up when he thought about the scene in the mobile home. How could someone do that to another human being?

He drank some more of his coffee and made his way into the interrogation room were the young girl sat. He lit a cigarette. "Mind if I smoke, Ms....."

Silence. She stared straight at the double sided glass, her eyes as wide as they were the previous night. Her face seemed to sag like a prune in the fluorescent light. He walked over to the empty chair that sat across from her and sat down, her gaze unmoving. Turner laid both of his arms on the table and looked her in the eyes. A sudden sense of uneasiness came over him as his gaze met hers. They say the portal to a person's soul is through the eyes. If that was the case, Turner wondered if this young lady had one.

"What's your name, sweetie? I'm here to..."

Before he could finish she grabbed his arms and jerked him closer. Her strength reminded him of a lumberjack. She stared at him for a second and gave a deep belly laugh that bounced off of the walls. Then she pressed her nose up against his. Her breath reeked of dried blood. When she opened her mouth to speak he could see tiny morsels of flesh sitting between her teeth. Turner tried to jerk away but her fingers dug into his arms like a clamp being tightened. He could hear a deep groan in her throat before she spoke.

"He came and stood by me as I gutted the whores. He came like he said, through the portal on the floor. The time has come for his return. He's coming for you, detective, and you are going to burn!"

Turner couldn't shake the eerie feeling as she spoke. He struggled and fought against her grip until she finally let go. Then she crumpled to the floor and cried. Big wailing gasps that haunted the room and the area behind the double sided glass.

Turner gathered himself, "Okay, I'm done, guys. You can have her."

He stumbled out of the room, grabbed his jacket and went straight to his car.

Driving was good therapy for Turner. With the window rolled down and the music cranked up, he thought about the odd feeling he had in the room with the young girl. She must have been a little coherent. She referred to him as detective. *How did she know that?* He hadn't mentioned his name nor showed her his badge. And her stout grip had taken him by surprise.

He had to go home and clear his mind. Maybe he'd call Ross and see what he was doing tonight. It would be good to have someone over, maybe have a drink or two to help with the edge. Ross would understand.

Turner drove, thinking about the last twenty-four hours. "Looks like a system is moving in from the south of us and we could see some heavy downpours with potential cell activity. The weather board has issued a tornado watch until nine p.m. tonight. Again a tornado..." Turner switched off the radio and sighed. Up ahead he could see the dark-blue storm clouds forming against the horizon. He wanted to enjoy the sunset on his drive. Maybe another time.

The sudden downpour took Turner by surprise as he pulled into the driveway. He slammed his door shut and ran inside. He flicked the lights on, threw his keys onto the counter, went to the refrigerator and grabbed a beer. He wanted to watch some television but the lightning flashes stopped him in his tracks. He decided the radio would suffice. The soothing sounds of Sade's "Smooth Operator" pulsed throughout the house as Turner went to his laptop and switched it on. He pulled up the photos of the crime scene that had haunted him during his drive home. She had to of had an accomplice. That sort of precision takes someone with a...

One of the pictures caught his eye has he scrolled through them. The pentagram on the floor had an ominous presence about it. Most religious nut jobs always referred to something similar, but of all of the ones he had worked, none of them had painted one in blood. Human blood, for that matter. He studied the picture of the symbol closer hoping to find something. Then it hit him. In the interrogation room the young girl had made a reference to something on the floor. A portal. Could she have been talking about the pentagram? Turner leaned back in his chair and laughed at the thought. Really, Turner?

You actually believe something came through that thing on the floor? That's just...

A heavy knock came from the front door.

Turner sat upright in his chair and looked at his watch. The wind howled as the inclement weather bore down its wrath. When he opened the door, there was no one there. He stepped out onto the porch and looked around. Only his car sat in the driveway, pelted by the torrential downpour. "I must be hearing things," he mumbled, trying to reassure himself.

He had just switched the laptop back on and opened up the case files when the phone rang. He glanced at the caller ID. The station was trying to ring through. This bothered him. It had to be an emergency if they were calling. Turner picked up the receiver. "Hello?"

"Turner! Thank goodness you're home. Listen, we had the girl transported to the mental ward in Pleasant Hill. We received a distress call from the officers transporting her. They've had an accident. I've called for an ambulance but they gave an ETA of twenty minutes. I hate to ask but can you go make sure the guys are okay and take the girl to the mental ward? I've got all units out on other calls."

Turner ran his fingers through his hair. "Okay. I'm on my way."

He hung up the phone, grabbed his jacket and ran out the front door.

The wind shook the small SUV as the detective sped towards the scene, jostling it like an empty tin can.

The squad car sat on its top, shards of glass littering the road. Turner parked his vehicle, grabbed his flashlight and hurried over to the upturned vehicle. Peering inside he could see the two officers still buckled in their seats, their faces covered in blood. Fearing the worst, he reached in to take a pulse, hoping they were okay, when he felt something odd on the driver's neck.

A slit. Not just any slit. Turner moved his flashlight onto the driver and looked for the gash. He saw a large opening from one ear to the other, like a gutted fish. Turner pulled back in disgust and quickly radioed for help. "Dispatch, come in? Anybody...I have two officers down and the suspect they were transporting is missing, over."

The only reply he got was the soft hush of static. "Damn it! Did anybody copy, over?"

More static followed by a high frequency squeal. Turner threw his radio down and ran back to his vehicle. He had to get some help. Just as he started the engine he saw a set of headlights coming up behind him. *Oh, good. Help is here.* Before he could get out, the mysterious vehicle slammed into the rear end of his SUV and sent it careening into the ditch, his head slamming into the steering wheel. Just before he lost consciousness, he saw a small figure walk up to his door and peer in. She motioned for someone to come over. A dark looming figure approached the door and the smell of sulfur and burnt matches filled his nostrils. The door opened and everything went dark.

Mozart played softly in the background and the smell of spices and herbs tickled Turners nose as he came to. A headache formed in his temples and behind his eyes. He squinted trying to figure out where he could be. He started to rub his eyes but realized he couldn't due to the thick rope that bound them to the chair he was sitting in. His blurred vision dissipated as he wrestled the rope, burning his elbows and biceps. The pain ran up and down both arms. When he couldn't free his arms, he screamed into the tape that covered his mouth.

The oak table that sat in front of him was dressed with a black and white tablecloth and adorned with an assortment of various meats. Four other people sat at the table with him, also. All wearing the same color and expression. And he recognized everybody. The three girls from yesterday's crime scene sat to the right of him, their mouths hanging open like a gate unhinged. To the left of him sat Stedam, the owner of the trailer park, with the same sickening look.

All four of the bodies had the same cut running from their neck to the lower abdomen. They had been gutted, hollowed out and stuffed.

Turner shook in his chair.

After a few moments, the teenaged suspect walked in and seated herself at the table. Before Turner could mumble, she began to eat from the assortment of meats. Then a tall, dark figure walked into the room. His gray, three-piece suit smoldered with smoke. Turner could make out the strong smell of sulfur. He started to mumble when the figure spoke.

"Hello, Detective Turner. I guess you have a lot of questions right now. I don't want to tarry too long so I'll cut to the chase. You see, Lisa needed some help with a few problems. Three bullies from school made her life a living hell. A man made her do things while her father was away on business. So she called on me. Now, you've stuck your nose in our business and we can't have that. So you are going to be the newest member to the collection."

The figure gave a soft, maniacal chuckle. He stood with his hands folded and nodded towards the young girl.

Turner's panic turned into fear. What did he mean "newest member"? Is he the accomplice? Then all thoughts left his mind. All wondering about the figure ceased. All he could think of now was the vibrating hum of the electric bone saw and the blistering, white-hot pain as it entered his chest.

About the author

Anthony Parker is a short story author and proud father of two. His work has been included in The Storyteller, December 2013 and a non-fiction piece in a company newsletter titled Spotlight. When he's not frightening his friends with his writing, he's most likely frightening his wife or mother. His short term goal is to have more short stories published within the year. His long term goal is to have a novel written by next year.

~~ © 2015 The Collection/Anthony Parker

THE FIRST SOUND YOU HEAR

Bruce Memblatt

The first bullet didn't sound like a bullet at all. Pete thought it was the sound of a car backfiring in the snowy street below, muffled but clearly a car. At night things always sounded different, particularly on winter nights when wind and snow could conspire to change everything.

But there are things that can't be changed.

He turned away from the window because he heard it again. This time clearer, not coming from the enchanted streets below, but from the sterile bathroom across the hall. The sound was followed by the sound of footsteps running, a door opening, and then the worst sound he ever heard, the worst sound anyone ever heard, his mother's scream, "Dear God, no, Bill!"

Ten year old Pete threw open his bedroom door to see blood dripping streaming across the hall, his mother kneeling in it, crouched over his father's corpse, a gun in her shaking hand, crying, "How could you do this to us, Bill?"

That's when everything stopped.

That was the moment the magic died forever and Pete somehow knew along with his father his child-hood died too, though he could not name the empty regretful feeling at the time.

He told himself sometimes you just know as he stared at the gun shaking in his mother's hand. Maybe if he wasn't so smart. What good would his high IQ do him now? He listened to the sad cries coming from somewhere deep in his mother's bel-ly, and he heard her call, "Come here, Pete. Please, help me up. We have to call the police. I don't un-derstand. Why did he kill himself? Why? How could this be happening? It can't be happening!"

Then Pete stood staring, shaking without and within and all that came from his throat were the words, "but the gun is in your hand, Mommy." It was, it was in her hand. It still was in her hand. Pete knew it was an image that would never leave his mind like that time he saw his friend Jimmy dive into the pool, miss, and slam his head into the concrete; blood was everywhere, just like tonight.

His mother, Sarah, turned towards him and toss-ing the gun to the blood-soaked parquet beneath them, she said, "I picked it up from the floor, Pete.

It must have fallen from your father's hand after he pulled the trigger."

Of course, what was wrong with him? Mommy loved daddy.

They cooed all the time like birds, but wait a second...Pete jumped, hardly able to contain himself because he watched enough TV to know you're not supposed to touch the evidence.

"But Mommy," he cried, " your prints are on the gun now!"

"It's okay, Pete we'll just tell them I accidentally picked it up in all the commotion."

He sighed. "To be sure Mommy, I'll tell them I saw you pick it up."

"But you know you shouldn't lie, Pete."

"Just this time. We've been through enough."

His mother half-smiled as she sniffled, wiped the last tears out of her eye, and said, "Okay, Pete, just this once, thanks my little man."

Then he felt her arms wrapping around his shoulders like soft blankets and for a moment he felt safe. The world was still a place he could trust.

But like things always seemed to happen, it was then that he heard it again.

The sound he heard before in the street. The sound of the car backfiring. He knew his mother heard it too, because her arms jumped from his shoulders like springboards, exposing them to the cold air, and his eyes to the sudden chill on her face.

"That's nothing, Pete, just a car in the street."

"I heard it before, Mommy. Not long before I heard the gun," Pete said and then he jumped, and ran back in his room; back to the window because he heard footsteps in the snow, but before he could catch a look, a new sound shocked his ears.

The front door downstairs; first a rapping on the glass, then the creaky sneak of the door opening.

Scrambling, Pete was trying to catch his breath when he saw his mother running into his room, nervously tightening her shirt around her waist. "Don't worry, Pete it will be okay."

The awful chill was still in her stare; the look that changed her eyes when they heard the sound in the snow.

He looked up at her and said, "Weren't you going to call the police, Mommy?"

He hated the accusatory tone in his voice. He hated everything about this night.

"In a moment, in a moment, Pete."

Mommy's eyes were even weirder now like she was lost in an odd dance.

He could hear the footsteps below coming closer. They both could as whoever was in their house began to climb the stairs.

Pete stared at his mother, and she stared back at him. They couldn't move. They were locked, paralyzed in a strange shock. The footsteps became even louder. He wanted to breathe, he wanted to run, he wanted to scream but all he could do was look at mommy and hope there was an answer in her faraway eyes.

He pushed his fists in the air and inside he cried *Make all this go away, God please reverse this!*

Then a young man, tall, lean, wearing a thick coat burst into Pete's room. Pete saw the look of recognition and shock in his mother's eyes, the tremble in her hands that were now trying to cover her face, the tears that ran down her cheeks as she stammered out the name, "Bill."

But Bill was daddy's name and daddy was lying on the floor in a pool of...

Suddenly Sarah screamed, "My God, what is happening!"

Did he do this? How... He stared at his mother's eyes again and he whispered, "Is that daddy?"

"Yes, Pete, yes, but when he was young. That's what he looked like when we first met."

She continued to stare at the man. He was standing still, just gazing at Pete and Sarah.

"Why isn't he speaking, Mommy? Mommy what is going on? I'm scared. I'm so scared!"

He didn't even know how he managed to get the words out. He just stood shaking and watched.

The young man moved closer, brushed his fine black hair with his hands, straightening it out like he was preparing for a date. Then he reached into his coat pocket and pulled out a box of chocolates wrapped in a red ribbon.

Sarah's eyes halted like they recognized the box, then she whispered to Pete. "There's nothing to be afraid of, angel, see that box of candy in his hand? That's what he brought me on our first date. That's how he looked. My God, that's what he wore!"

Pete scrambled to his mother's side and tugged on her legs, "But today isn't your first date, Mommy! And Daddy is lying on the floor over there!"

He wondered what his mother was thinking; it was as if she were a stick, or a leaf tossing in the breeze, unable to pull herself away from the power the imitation daddy had over her.

He watched her eyes turn even dreamier as she stared at the man, who still stood in Pete's room strangely gazing at them; that box of candy still dangling from his hands.

Then she called to Pete, "That sound we heard before? Now I remember it. When your father pulled into the driveway on our first date his car backfired, that old car of his always..."

"Mommy, please wake up! This isn't a long time ago this is now!"

"It was a Chevy an old white Chevy."

It couldn't possibly be the same car, Pete told himself. He had to see. He ran to the window.

He shuddered. The car was there too, "My God," he cried, almost tripping to the floor as the white vehicle filled his vision.

There it was just as mom described it, but it shined in the soft snowy glare of the streetlight like it had just been waxed. As he stared at his father's car every nerve in his body heightened to the point that he knew if he didn't calm down something bad would happen to him.

How would he ever get back to the world he loved? If only he could turn back the clock. But that was the problem now wasn't it? He thought as he watched his young father approach his star-crossed mother.

He had to stop them. He had to wake mommy up. He ran back to her and tugged on her oversized night shirt.

The shutters nearly flew off the window in the small boy's wake.

"Mommy, please you have to listen to me," he cried, but it was as if he wasn't there, like he was a ghost or a sliver of dust.

Unshaken, his mother began to move towards the man.

There had to be something he could say or do to wake her. Then it came to him, and he rushed towards her shouting, "Weren't you going to call the police, Mommy? Maybe, I should. Maybe I will, and perhaps I'll tell them about how the gun was in your hand?"

He hated himself for saying it. He wanted to vomit and cleanse his throat of the vile it just spewed, but he had to do something, and it seemed to work. His mother turned away from his young father and began to walk back towards Pete quickly and deliberately.

He cautiously smiled as she approached him.

Then he felt the cold slap she gave him across his face, raw and hard, and he began to cry.

"You won't call the police, Pete, and you won't threaten me! Do you hear me?" She said with her hand in position near his face, Pete knew, ready to slap him again if he didn't surrender.

My god, he cried inside, who was this? It couldn't possibly be his mother.

It wasn't. It was just everything. Everything was wrong and strange and sad...

But, suddenly, in his ears like a rescue, there was music, beautiful lilting music playing. And they turned their heads as the man, Pete's younger father, neared Sarah and took her hand.

Then she said, teasing her hair with her fingers almost giddy," I recognize this music. This is the song we danced to that first night, Stranger in Paradise from Kismet!"

At once, Pete's ears trembled to the sound of his father's voice breaking through the room; his father's voice younger and purer, "That's right, Honey. I had them play that song just for us."

Pete saw his father gaze into his mother's eyes, and he was swept away into the illusion too. He stood and dreamily gazed as they wrapped their arms around each other and began to dance.

It was as if the boy's small room turned into a hall. He could almost see the crystal lights in his eyes, like a fairy tale was unfolding around him. And he watched them spin and, turn and dance. And it was so beautiful, he thought, maybe there was still a chance, maybe not in the world he knew but in this new world.

Was it possible, could they stay there? Did it matter? They were there now with beautiful music; his parents both still alive spinning soaring, flying wrapped around each other like magic.

They began to speak. Pete watched on in an absent stare.

Sharon cuffed the back of Bill's neck and whispered in his ear, "This is how it used to be, Bill, remember just like a dream."

He dipped her and said, "Just like a dream. We were living in a wonderful dream, Sarah."

The music crescendoed and they twirled round and round and round.

"We thought it would never end," Sarah said.

Bill laughed, "What fools we were!"

"The worst! "Sarah laughed too.

"I still love you, Sarah."

"And I you, Bill, no matter what I will always love you!"

She smiled. Her teeth sparkled as Bill dipped her again.

"Then why did you kill me, darling?"

"Because," she giggled, "and why did you cheat on me?"

Bill smiled wide, "because I was bored."

Once again the music soared, and they magically spun and spun around like they were dancing on air.

Pete still watched on, a grin on his face, like he was the happiest boy in the world.

"Look at him, Sarah, he's so happy. Have you ever seen him so happy?"

"If he only knew, Bill," she laughed as she wrapped her arms around his neck.

He playfully pulled at her fingers, "yes, if he only knew, but one thing, Sarah, your big mistake was he saw you with the gun."

"What's the diff," she grinned, "I explained everything.

He believed me. That's all that matters. After all I couldn't let you leave me, leave us. Then where would Pete be?" She smiled.

Bill dipped her again. The music became louder. Very loud.

Pete's stare suddenly changed. Something was wrong. Their dancing was becoming awkward. The music was veering out of control.

He looked closer and then he noticed it first in his father's eyes. They were changing, aging.

Mommy must have noticed it too, because she began to stammer and scream.

Dear God, daddy was becoming old before his eyes. Daddy was starting to look like himself and he was pulling on mommy hard. He was trying to hurt her.

She screamed again. Then Daddy's hands wrapped around her throat.

Pete hollered, and he charged towards his parents like a bullet.

But Daddy was strangling Mommy.

Pete cried, "Stop, please Daddy stop!"

Then Mommy kicked him hard, and Daddy started to fall.

Mommy got away!

Pete gasped as he saw his mother run towards the hall.

Then daddy ran after her. Fast, dear God so fast.

Pete scrambled and just made it to the doorway. There he heard gun shots in the hallway right outside his room.

Just like before.

He barreled out into the hall, and he saw his mother and father lying in a deep pool of blood. It was-it was just like before.

He stood and he shook and tears came. He thought they'd come forever.

Ten minutes later he picked up the phone and called the police.

Five more minutes had passed when he heard the sirens.

He ran back to his room and gazed out the window. His father's black car sat in the driveway like it did every night, now surrounded by police cars and the frenzied red whirl of the sirens lighting the snow.

There was no way back.

In the distance he heard a car backfire.

About the author

Bruce Memblatt resides in a small apartment in the Rego Park section of Queens in New York City. He has lived in New York City all his life. He has studied Business Administration at Pace University. He has worked as an accountant, a dispatcher in an auto shop, a filing clerk for Mercedes Benz, and even as a piano player in a small café that was called The Inner Circle in Greenwich Village in the mid-1980s, among other things.

He is a member of the Horror Writers Association, and he is on the staff of The Horror Zine as Kindle Coordinator

His short story, "Dikon's Light," is a recipient of Bewildering Stories 2012 Mariner Awards.

His short story "Destination Unknown," received an honorable mention in the 2012 L. Ron Hubbard Writers of the Future Awards.

His short story Wish Upon an Indifferent Clearing was published in FORGOTTEN PLACES: BEST OF THE HORROR SOCIETY 2014

And his short story "Hard Rain," is featured in the recent best-selling anthology from Post Mortem Press and The Horror Zine, SHRIEKS AND SHIVERS.

His works have been published several times in anthology books, magazines and zines such as

Aphelion, Nameless Magazine (Cycatrix Press), Suspense Magazine, Post Mortem Press, Dark Moon Books, Sam's Dot Publishing, Strange Weird and Wonderful Magazine, The Horror Zine, Midwest Literary Magazine, Danse Macabre, Parsec Ink, The Feathertale Review, Yellow Mama and many more.

From 2010 to 2014 he penned a bi-weekly series for The Piker Press based on his short story, "Dinner with Henry."

Mainly a writer of short horror and dark fiction stories he plans to start work on a novel very soon.

~~ ©2015   The First Sound You Hear/Bruce Memblatt

BIZARRE TALES OF HORROR

THE LADY IN ORANGE

Patrick McKinney

It has been widely assumed ghosts are the product of residual energy left over from beings that inhabited a particular area sometime in the past. What if that were only partially true...?

The Eastern Ohio Ghost Guys had been investigating paranormal sightings for several years but this would be their first opportunity to investigate a home in Wheeling, West Virginia. Its rich history dating back to the early 1800's made Wheeling the perfect location for paranormal activity. This could be their big break! Not taking any chances the four men brought their newest "state of the art" equipment they had purchased for an investigation like this.

The unpredictable northern West Virginia weather had turned from a sunny cloudless morning to a gloomy overcast afternoon as the team crossed the Ohio River onto Wheeling Island. They drive several blocks then turn right heading south on the island.

As they turn onto the street they are completely blown away. On both sides of the street are massive Victorian and Queen Anne houses. The mansions are testament to the fortunes made in the area during the mid-nineteenth century. After several minutes they find the house they have been invited to investigate. It is a tall dark and imposing three story brick structure. The unique architectural style combines a mansard roof with several jutting gables and a tall square tower reminiscent of a castle keep.

When they reach the house they notice a small middle aged woman sitting on the porch. The guys climb the steps up the rise the house sits on to the large front porch that runs across half the front of the mansion and wraps around the right side.

"Looks like a storm's blowin' up," she says as they walk up the steps.

Dan, the head of the group replied, "Sure does! It came up all of a sudden. We are the Eastern Ohio Ghost Guys. You must be Dorothy."

"That's right. You boys ready to meet my ghost?" she smiled.

With that the five of them walked through the large double front doors into the house. Inside Dorothy showed the guys the massive main staircase. Six feet wide, it climbed from the center of the main hall just inside the front door to a large stained glass window on the second floor at the back of the house.

"This is where I see her. The Lady in Orange," Dorothy announced. She went on to explain the Lady in Orange is an orange shaded mist that people have seen drifting down the steps. "I've seen it many times myself!" she said. Through her own investigating Dorothy found that one of the first owners of the mansion had a daughter named Ophelia. They lived here during the late 1880's or 1890's. Dorothy also found that Effie, as she liked to be called, was known for almost always wearing elaborate orange Victorian gowns.

"I know it's her," Dorothy said, "because certain times if you call for Effie you can see the orange mist float down the steps!"

Effie was the 23 year old daughter of a prominent Wheeling businessman who amassed a fortune in a local glassworks. Being born into privilege she was able do and be whatever she pleased.so Effie, being a free spirit chose not to conform to the dark stuffy dress of the period. Instead she would wear bright orange dresses with plenty of feathers and décor, so much so she became known around Wheeling as "The Lady in Orange."

When Effie became of age she was able to further her education at finishing school in Boston. While there she became interested in the Victorian obsession with death and séances. Almost every night she would join friends, and a medium, around a table attempting to conjure whatever spirits they could find. Usually nothing came of the event but on occasion Effie was certain the medium had made some type of contact with the other side.

When she returned to Wheeling she sought out mediums to perform séances at the mansion for her and her friends. During one of these séances the medium told Effie that she would soon be contacted by entities from another time. They would come through a portal of lights and they would know her by name! Shocked by the mediums prognostication, Effie stopped the séances and put thoughts of death and spirits out of her mind.

Several weeks passed and one night during a particularly nasty thunderstorm Effie was in her room and thought she heard someone downstairs. She came out of her room and walked to the top of the stairway. Looking down the stairs she could see the occasional flicker of a light and what sounded like a person mumbling.

"Who is there?" she asked. But there was no response.

The light was flickering a little brighter so Effie decided to take a few steps down the stairs to get a closer look. As she walked down the steps the light turned to several flickering lights. They were getting closer and the mumbling voices seemed to be getting closer too!

Effie was about halfway down the stairs. The lights coming up the steps had gotten even brighter. And now she thought she could make out what one of the voices was saying. She listened closer to make sure. It was, the voice was saying her name! She could hear it clearly now. Effie...Effie, is that you. She felt her knees starting to give as she frantically asked, "Who is there?"

But wait! Looking up from bottom of the stairs we are given a different perspective. From here we see Dan and the other Ghost Guys climbing the stairs. They are aiming flashing strobe devices up the stairway that are supposed attract paranormal energy. Another is holding a recording device that has picked up a voice asking "Who is there?" Coming down the staircase they see the orange mist that Dorothy told them about. And Dan begins asking, "Effie, is that you?"

...could we be witness to scenes from our future... or a parallel timeline?

About the author

Patrick was born and raised in Ohio, has traveled throughout the United States and Canada, and currently resides in Virginia. He enjoys writing, photography, and traveling. He is currently working on his first novel, yet to be named, and hopes to publish in within the next year.

BIZARRE TALES OF HORROR

THE TOOTH FAIRY

Rie Sheridan Rose

"Mom...there's something I have to tell you..."
Louise looked up from the laundry she was folding.

Bryan stood in the doorway, a worried frown on his face.

He was so serious for a six-year-old. He looked like a little old man in his khakis and button-down shirt—his choice; she'd given up trying to get him into a tee-shirt and jeans.

"What is it, baby?"

He rolled his eyes.

"I'm sorry, I forgot, you're not a baby anymore. What do you need?"

He held out a shaking hand. In the center of his palm was one of his front teeth. He'd finally lost one.

"Look at that! It's okay, sweetie." She smiled at him. "Everyone loses their baby teeth eventually. Just goes to show you're right. You're growing up." She knelt in front of him, closing his fingers around the tooth. "Put it under your pillow tonight and see what happens. You know what they say about the tooth fairy."

Bryan shook his head, "I don't want to."

"Don't you want the tooth fairy to come visit?"

He shook his head more vigorously, "Nope."

"Why not?" Louise was astonished her practical son would turn down any chance for a bit of cash.

"It'll bite me." His face was white as a sheet.

"Where did you hear that?" Louise bit back the desire to laugh that rose to her lips. It was such an odd thing to say. But from the look on his face, he was totally serious. Where had he picked up such a notion?

"Freddie lost a tooth, and the next day, he came to school with a big chunk out of his arm. He said the tooth fairy bit him. Pete lost both his front teeth when he fell at recess, and he never came back to school at all—because he was dead."

"Honey, I'm sure Freddie was just teasing you... and didn't Pete's family move to Denver?"

"Yeah, but Pete didn't go with them. Marcy knows his sister Vickie, and Vickie told her they were moving away, because her Mom and Dad couldn't stand to be in the same town where Pete was eaten to death."

"And when did Marcy tell you this?"

"Yesterday."

"Did you tell her you had a loose tooth?"

Bryan nodded miserably.

"I see. Well, don't you worry about a thing," Louise patted her son's shoulder. "I'll just have a talk with Marcy. I bet, between us, we can convince the nice tooth fairy to come visit you tonight."

Bryan didn't look convinced, but he offered her a weak smile, putting the tooth into the pocket of his shirt.

"I guess it'll be okay, then. If you promise it won't hurt me."

Louise hunkered down before him again, taking his hand. "Sweetie, I promise. The tooth fairy won't hurt you. You leave it to me."

His face brightened with the trust of a child for his mother. The smile widened into his customary grin—with an engaging gap in the front. "Okay, Mom. I'm going to go show Freddie."

"Good boy. Just be home in time for dinner. About an hour, okay?"

"Sure." He turned and ran for the front door.

As soon as she heard the door shut behind him, Louise went to the bottom of the stairs. "Marcela Olivia Cantrell, get down here immediately."

"What?"

"Don't 'what' me, young lady! Get your butt down here."

She could hear the sigh of exasperation through Marcy's closed door. But her sixteen-year-old knew better than to push her luck, and the girl slumped her way down the stairs to stand just out of reach.

"Yeah? What is it now?"

"Did you or did you not tell your little brother that his friend Pete was eaten by the tooth fairy?"

Marcy was instantly nervous. Her entire body shrank in on itself as she nodded, "It's true."

Louise vented her own sigh of exasperation. "You know that's absolutely ridiculous. Why did you want to spoil the tooth fairy for him?"

"No, Mom. It's true! Vickie was my best friend. Do you think I'd make up something so horrible? She told me her little brother was chewed to bits in his bed. Right after he put his front teeth under his pillow. They moved away because her parents couldn't stand to be in the house anymore. She didn't even get to tell me goodbye in person—she had to send me a text. They left the next day. Honest!"

"That is the stupidest story I've ever heard. People would be talking about it all over town if it were true. I don't know why Vickie lied to you like that, but it sounds like you're better off without her. Now, when your brother gets home, I want you to tell him you were only teasing—playing a joke on him. You hear me?"

"But Mom..."

"You tell him it was made-up, or you can forget about going to that concert next weekend."

"But I have tickets!"

"Then you'd better convince him you were lying, hadn't you? And don't you ever fill his head with monsters again. You know how impressionable he is."

"Yes, ma'am." Marcy turned to go back to her room then paused, with her hand on the banister. "I'll tell him what you want me to tell him...but I really didn't make it up. And I don't think Vickie was lying."

She ran up the stairs and into her room, slamming the door behind her.

Louise threw up her hands. "What the hell is going on?"

She thought a moment then marched into the kitchen to pick up the phone.

Dialing from memory, she waited for the connection to be made.

She'd get to the bottom of this once and for all.

"Hello?" The voice on the other end of the phone was slightly breathless, as if the owner had run to answer it.

"Hi, Carol. I didn't mean to catch you at a bad time."

"No problem, Louise. Just trying to get in a bit of treadmill while the boys were occupied. What's up?"

"I know this is going to sound a bit crazy, but Bryan said Freddie came to school with a bite mark on his arm the other day. I was just wondering if you could tell me what happened."

"It was the darnedest thing, Lou. I really don't know. I swear. He went to bed fine, and a little after midnight he started screaming. Daryl and I ran in to see what was going on, and he was sitting up in bed with blood streaming down his arm. There was a definite bite on his arm, but no one was in the room but Freddie. All we can figure is that he did it himself in his sleep. He denies it, of course."

"Does he have a history of sleep disorder?"

"No, but Doctor Morrow seemed to think it was a valid explanation. Certainly better than 'the tooth fairy attacked me' which is what he kept saying," Carol Hollister laughed. To Louise, the laugh sounded rather brittle.

"Well, don't let Bryan make a pest of himself. He knows he's supposed to be home by supper."

"Bryan's an angel—I just wish he'd rub off on Freddie! Don't worry. I'll send him home when the kids are through with the video they are watching."

"Thanks, Carol. Talk to you later."

Louise hung up the phone more confused than ever. The idea of a cannibalistic tooth fairy was just ridiculous. But something was definitely going on here. Maybe she should check the internet to see if any of these "bites" had been in the news. Surely, if there were children being killed like this, there would be something posted. The police blotter would say something if nothing else.

An hour later, she was more confused than ever. While there were no overt references to bite injuries to local children, there had been a rash of strange occurrences lately. The police seemed to be treating it as some sort of serial attacker. There was even a curfew for anyone under the age of twenty—she'd have to keep an eye on Marcy.

But it had to be something reasonable...a human explanation, no matter how heinous. And if it were a human, she could protect her children. No reason not to go through with the tooth fairy ritual.

She hated to deny Bryan the childhood pleasure of waking up in the morning and finding money under his pillow...which reminded her. She'd better check her wallet and make sure she had some cash.

When she was a girl, the tooth fairy had left a quarter for a tooth, and it had seemed like a fortune. With Marcy, she and Rob had decided a dollar bill was more appropriate, given inflation.

She chuckled to herself. "Better see if I have a five."

###

Later that evening, after Bryan had gone to bed with his tooth under his pillow, and Marcy was closeted in her room, Louise told her husband about the odd stories the children had told her that afternoon.

"Honestly, Rob, Bryan was terrified by the thought of the tooth fairy. Can you believe it? The tooth fairy!"

"Hell, I used to hurry along every tooth that started to wiggle," Rob grinned. "I don't know how many times I wrestled with a tooth until it gave up and fell out. He'll be fine, honey. It's just the first one. Wait till he sees that five you have for him. He'll start testing them all daily."

Reassured, Louise smiled back, "You're probably right. Mercenary little fella, isn't he? He gets that from your side of the family." She poked him in the ribs.

"It's a good thing one of us is responsible in this family," he replied with a wink.

Rob could always make her feel better. No doubt he was right. Just one of those little quirks of childrearing...one her own mother had forgot to mention.

They settled down in front of the television with a bottle of wine and a movie. By the time both had finished, Louise was sure Carol Hollister had been pulling her leg and Vickie Brown had been performing a similar maneuver on Marcy. The police would handle the all-too human threat roaming the streets, and Bryan would eventually forget all about his fear of the tooth fairy.

"He's probably asleep by now," she told Rob. "I'm going to go up and leave the money now."

"Let's go together. Just in case the tooth monster tries to get you." He made a grotesque face and Louise laughed.

She stuck her tongue out at him. "All right, Mister Smarty-Pants. You can come too—but I get to put the money under his pillow."

"You always get to have all the fun," he pouted.

She laughed, linking her arm through his. "Damn straight, Skippy."

As they headed up the stairs, Louise was overwhelmed by how blessed she was: she had a husband who she adored, and who loved her equally; a teenage daughter who had never been involved in any of the petty trouble her friends sometimes got into; and a brilliant little boy who might just grow up to be the next president. Who could ask for more?

When they reached Bryan's door, it was shut.

Louise turned to Rob with a frown. "He never shuts his door at night. That's a Marcy thing. Bryan's still afraid of the dark."

"Maybe he's decided it really is time he grew up a little," Rob shrugged. "You know, 'today I became a man' sort of thing."

"I don't like it." She reached for the doorknob. It was ice cold beneath her hand. "What the—?"

Throwing open the door, she started into the room then fell back into Rob's arms with a cry.

A figure crouched over Bryan's bed, limned by moonlight from the window behind it.

"W-what is going on...?" Louise whimpered.

The figure straightened, turning toward them. Its head almost brushed the ceiling, and it seemed to have more appendages than appropriate. The blob where its head should be was misshapen, and its teeth glowed in the ambient light.

Louise slammed a hand into the light switch, breaking a nail in the process. Light flooded the room. And she wished to God it had not.

Bryan's bed was awash with blood. He hung askew on the mattress, one hand trailing the floor, his head almost severed from his body. Her beautiful child...

The thing looming over the bed was huge, sprouting three sets of arms from its scaled, leathery hide.

A necklace formed of teeth looped several times about its neck, and each meaty wrist was encircled by a ring of molars. Almost as many teeth seemed to fill its blood-soaked snout.

Louise screamed.

Whirling, Rob shoved her out of the room. "Get Marcy. Get Out!"

She fell back against the far wall of the hallway— frozen to the spot.

"Get out!" Rob shouted. "Get out of the house! I'll get Bryan."

Lunging forward, she grabbed his arm. "Rob— he's dead, Bryan is dead. We have to get out of here." Louise sobbed, straining to hold him back.

"Let me go, Louise! I have to save my son. Get Marcy and get her out of here." Jerking free of her hold, he started forward.

The creature met him halfway across the room, tearing his throat out with its sharp incisors.

Louise screamed again.

"Mom...?" Marcy's voice was blurred with sleep. "What's going on?"

The sound of Marcy's voice broke the spell on Louise. She had to save her daughter before it was too late. She spun on her heel and started down the hall. Marcy stood in her doorway, rubbing the sleep from her eyes.

There was a searing pain as something attached itself to her shoulder. Louise jerked away, stumbling forward. Warm blood poured down her arm. She could feel the creature's hot breath on her back. "Run, Marcy, run!" she ordered, as hands gripped all four limbs and began to pull.

Marcy turned and ran. The stairs were only a few feet away, and terror lent her feet wings. She never looked back.

Time blurs all pain. Two decades had passed since the murders of her family. Marcy had never forgotten that night. She hadn't seen the creature that killed her parents and brother...but she had a pretty good idea what it had been considering the events leading up to that night of horror.

Somehow, she had managed to move on with her life eventually. Marrying her college sweetheart, becoming a mother, all the things she wished she could have shared with Louise and Rob. Bryan would have been such a great uncle to her children.

The kids were growing up so fast. Robin was almost eight, Louis six.

Marcy sighed, tucking away the photo album she had been leafing through. It was the only thing she'd kept from her past.

Enough reminiscing. Time to get dinner ready.

She was standing at the stove, adding spices to her famous spaghetti sauce when Robin stepped into the doorway.

"Mom!"

"What is it, sweetie?"

"Mom, look!" The little girl held out her hand proudly. Centered on her palm was a tooth.

About the author

Rie Sheridan Rose has been writing since early childhood, when it was all in crayon and very hard to read. She has been at it professionally since the turn of the century, having seen her first novel release in 2000. She writes for a variety of small presses as well as editing chores for a couple. Rie really loves to write.

Rie's short stories appear in numerous anthologies, including Nightmare Stalkers and Dream Walkers Vols. 1 and 2, Come to My Window, Shifters, The Grotesquerie and In the Bloodstream as well as Yard Dog Press' A Bubba In Time Saves None. Yard Dog Press is also home to the humorous horror tales featuring Bruce and Roxanne—in the process of being collected into a trade paperback. Mocha Memoirs has "Drink My Soul...Please," and "Bloody Rain" as e-downloads—soon to be part of the short story collection RieTales, available at the end of March. Online, she has appeared in Cease, Cows, Lorelei Signal, and Four Star Stories.

Besides short stories, she is the author of six novels, five poetry chapbooks, and lyrics for songs on several of Marc Gunn's CDs. Her latest venture was editing the Steampunk Airship Pirates anthology Avast, Ye Airships! for Mocha Memoirs. Her next project is final edits on The Nearly Notorious Nun, the second book in the series The Conn-Mann Chronicles from Zumaya Publications.

She dabbles in most genres, with favorites in Steampunk and Horror at the moment, but that could change with her mood. Her first love is poetry, and she is on a mission to revive its popularity at conventions.

Rie lives in the heart of Texas with her husband and a wrangle of spoiled cats. When not writing, she is reading, playing video games, taking photographs, and avoiding housecleaning. You can find out more about her work on her website, www.. reiwriter.com or follow on Facebook. She tweets as @RieSheridanRose.

~~ © 2015 The Tooth Fairy/Rie Sheridan Rose

WELCOME HOME

J. Thayer McKinney

Kimberly Jordan had been the director of editing at Horror Publications for almost fifteen years. She took her job seriously and even decorated her corner office with the latest in authentic horror items. The art work on her walls were a mixture of horror, blood, and evil. She had a fireplace that looked like a demon with an open mouth. "All this horror memorabilia gives me motivation," she explained to anyone willing to listen.

Today she was going to her favorite antique haunts in search of a skull, and not just any skull, she wanted an authentic human skull.

"Don't you think it might be illegal to possess a human skull?" her co-worker asked.

"So what, if someone will sell me one, no one will ever know."

"I think its morbid to have human remains as decorations," he replied.

"You're just too sensitive and vanilla."

"I'm most certainly not vanilla!"

"Yes you are, you won't try anything or do anything you feel is the least bit reprehensible."

"I'm not vanilla," he muttered as he turned and left the office.

As she was walking through the antique district, she spotted a store she hadn't noticed before. It had a very unique name, Bizarre Needs. "Well Bizarre Needs, let's see if you live up to your name."

She walked into the shop and was immediately overcome with nostalgia. It seemed to ooze from everything. She was sure she had been transported back in time to a place of oddities. The shopkeeper surprised her as he came down the steps from the tiny office at the rear of the shop.

"Good afternoon, is there something I can help you find?"

"Hello, no, I'm just browsing, thank you," she said as she slowly walked around the shop.

He watched her for a few minutes and then walked over to a small display to the right of where she was looking.

"I believe this might be what you are looking for," the shopkeeper said holding a skull.

"That's exactly what I'm looking for. How did you know?"

"It's my job to know what my customers need."

"Is it a human skull?"

"Now you know it's illegal to sell human remains," he said with a wink and a sly grin.

"How much do you want for it?"

"This gem is $100 and I'll throw in the wooden pallet it's resting on."

"I'll take it. Do you take credit cards?"

"Cash only, please."

"No problem," she said as she dug into her purse.

The shopkeeper wrapped the skull and pallet and put them lovingly into a paper bag.

"Thank you for your patronage," he said with a slight bow as she took the parcel and walked out the door.

When she got back to the office, she was surprised to see that she'd been gone a little over 2 hours.

She took her treasure out of the bag, unwrapped it and set it and the pallet on a shelf near the window.

"Oh dear, I'm late for the meeting," she whispered as she looked at her watch.

She hurried to the conference room without picking up the folder with her notes, her notepad, or a pen.

As she took her seat, the CEO announced they were running a little late and wouldn't be starting the meeting for another few minutes.

Kimberly motioned her assistant over. "Jess, would you go down to my office and get the red folder from my desk and a notepad and pen?"

As Jess walked into her office, he noticed the skull sitting on her desk near the folder.

When he reached down the pick up the folder, the skull lurched and bit at his hand. He grabbed the folder and ran from the office.

When he entered the conference room, he was white as a sheet.

"Jess, what's wrong?" Kimberly asked.

"That skull in your office tried to bite me!" he said almost hysterical.

"Nonsense, the skull can't bite you. What are smoking?"

"I swear, when I reached down to pick up the folder, it tried to bite me."

"The skull was across the room on the stand by the window. It couldn't have tried to bite you."

"It was on the desk beside the folder."

Just then the CEO decided to open the meeting so they let it drop but Kimberly was curious about whether someone had moved the skull.

After the meeting, she took Jess by the arm and said, "Come on, let's check out this biting skull."

"I have other things to do. You can see for yourself that it's on your desk."

"No, you come with me and I'll prove to you that the skull didn't move and most certainly didn't try to bite you."

Reluctantly Jess followed her to the office. When they walked in, the skull was sitting on its pallet near the window.

"See, I told you it wasn't on my desk."

"It was while I was in here."

"You've been working in horror too long, you're starting to imagine things."

"I don't like that thing. Why did you get it anyway?"

"I think it gives the room a bit more of a horror atmosphere. After all, we do publish horror stories."

"We don't have to live them"

"Go ahead and get back to work. I'll have a talk with Mr. Skull and tell him to not bite the help," Kimberly laughed.

Jess sulked out of the office, upset that Kimberly didn't believe him. He was almost starting to not believe it himself.

That night, the custodian, a happy little old man, whistled as he dusted the floors in the outer cubicles. He carried the waste cans to the trash chute in the hallway and did a little jig as he emptied each of the cans. He had worked here for almost 3 years and hoped to work for 3 or 4 more until he was old enough to sign up for Medicare. It wasn't a difficult job and the hours he worked, no one was around to bother him.

When the outer cubicles were finished he started on the offices. His last office was Kimberly Jordan's. He loved cleaning Kimberly's office because she had some of the best horror decorations he had ever seen. He was quite a horror fan and would spend extra time cleaning her office just so he could look around.

He whistled a lively tune as he dusted each of the decorations, something he didn't do in the other offices or cubicles. He lingered longer than usual dusting the skull. He let his hands move over the skull, almost lovingly. "You are a lovely specimen," he said as he closed his eyes and let his mind wander.

Reluctantly, he left the skull and continued cleaning the office, stealing an occasional look at the skull. That's strange, I thought the skull was facing the other way, he thought to himself. I must be getting tired. He continued cleaning and stole another look at the skull but it wasn't on its pallet, it was on the desk. "What the...!"

Fear welled up in him as he started to back toward the door. Just as his hand reached for the door handle the skull flew through the air straight at him. It hit him in the chest with such force that he dropped to his knees. It continued pounding his chest as his heart beat faster and faster. He was screaming in pain and fear as the skull retreated to its place on the pallet.

He tried to get up but his heart seemed to explode in his chest. He grabbed his chest as he fell backwards, gurgled, and felt his life leaving his body.

The next day, when Kimberly walked into her office, she screamed at the sight on the floor.

She had never seen a dead body before and the sight of the custodian was more than she could handle.

"Help me someone!" she screamed. "Call 911!"

Jess came running in and almost fainted when he saw the body. "Is he dead?" he asked.

"I don't know, I'm not touching him!"

"I'll call 911. Let's get out of here," Jess finally said, almost in hysterics.

After about 10 minutes, the police and EMTs arrived and confirmed their suspicions. As he was being carried out on the cart, one of the EMTs told them it looked like he had suffered a heart attack. The police decided there was no foul play so they left with the ambulance.

"Well, that was exciting," Kimberly said looking around her office. "I suppose someone should alert his family. Jess, go down to HR to let them know what happened. I'm sure they have information on his next of kin."

"How can you be so nonchalant? A man just died in your office and you act like it's no big deal," Jess complained.

"It isn't a big deal, he was old and we didn't really know him. After all, we are in the horror business, deal with it."

Jess mumbled something as he turned a started towards HR.

Kimberly closed her office door and walked towards the window to look out at the city. She loved the view from her office. As she turned around to go to her desk, she noticed the skull seemed to turn.

"What the devil! My eyes must be playing tricks on me. No more wine on a work night."

As she moved closer to her desk, the skull jumped from its pallet and flew towards her. It stopped just inches from her face. Terrified, she started to back up. When she got to the window, the skull backed away and rushed towards her with such force she hit the window. The window suddenly gave way and she fell 20 stories to the sidewalk below.

A few minutes later, Jess returned. He saw the opening where the window once was and ran over to look out. Below he saw the crumbled corpse and a crowd gathering. As he turned to hurry down to the street below the skull once again left its pallet. Jess saw it out of the corner of his eye as it flew towards him. Instinctively he backed up, lost his footing and fell through the opening. People below screamed as he landed in a heap beside Kimberly.

The old shopkeeper hummed a tune as he walked down the stairs from his small apartment over the shop. He smiled as he smelled the slight odor of sulfur. "You're here Master!" he whispered happily. The master is pleased, he thought to himself, much relieved.

He switched on the shop lights at the bottom of the stairs and walked to the door. He did a little jig as he unlocked the door and turned the sign to read 'OPEN'. The sulfur smell got stronger as he slowly turned back to the shop.

There sitting in its rightful place was the skull. It seemed to radiate a peaceful glow as the old man gazed at it.

As he walked toward it, it turned slightly. He never took his gaze from it as he said, "Welcome home."

About the author

J. Thayer McKinney lives with her husband in a log home in the mountains of eastern West Virginia. She is a wife, mother, grandmother and great-grand-mother. Along with being a writer and a paranormal researcher, she is the CEO/Executive Editor at Cedar Loft Publishing.

She loosely bases some of her fiction writing on her paranormal research. So far, she has not encountered many malevolent spirits but before she does research she grounds herself for protection.

"You can never be too careful with the unknown!"

She is an ordained minister and holds a PhD in Metaphysical Parapsychology. She has also earned a Bachelor's degree in Business Administration and an Associate's degree in Electronics.

Prior to retiring from the corporate world, she had a very successful and rewarding technical career. She managed the IT department at a healthcare facility and prior to that position she was an industrial controls technician and a telecommunications technician for a power company.

When she isn't writing or working at her publishing company, she enjoys traveling, ghost hunting, or sitting on the front porch listening to the sounds of nature.

She has published two books, *Grave Vengeance: Esther's Story and Haunting of LaBelle: Back to Hell* and is working on her third, *Realm of Evil: Door to Perdition.*